ONE NIGHT STAND

L. MOONE

CONTENTS

CHAPTER ONE

The meeting has left me exhausted and wired. Although it went well and I've landed the project, I don't feel too excited about it. The new customer is the sort of type whom you could give the equivalent of a perfect sunset and yet he'd be tweaking the colors until there would be no magic left in it.

Ordinarily I don't entertain such people, my web design company had grown successful enough that I didn't need to accept that kind of drain on my energy levels. However, lately things have been tough, and the project is too big and prestigious to pass up. Fingers crossed, with Akhil's support I can pull it off; it would turn things around for me.

Finding him to manage a team of freelancers in India had been a godsend on many previous occasions. I'm sure he will be equally valuable this time around.

If I ever deserved a drink, now is the time. I need to shake this knotted feeling in my chest, before it drives me nuts. It'll turn out fine, as always...

When I'm out by myself, rather than enjoying a fancy dinner, I usually opt for something simple, portable. A kebab or something from the chip shop.

The rest of the evening will be spent whiling the hours away in the first decent-looking pub I can find.

And I've just found it.

As soon as I've found my seat of choice in the dimly lit establishment, I notice him. Sitting on a bar stool nursing a full pint while his two friends stand around waiting for their refills. They clearly arrived as a group, but while I observe them it quickly becomes clear that they are not planning to just sit at the bar together.

He's sporting a typical metal head ponytail, longer than my own hair and it really suits him. Too many guys can't get past their old faithful long hairstyle, even when their mane starts to thin. His hair is thick and full though and the first thing I noticed. I have always had a thing for men with long hair.

Chance brought me here tonight to the aptly named "Old Oak". Only a short walk from my hotel, its traditional wood paneled decor looks like the perfect environment to escape to.

It's the sort of place which you can imagine to have been here forever. Probably has done for hundreds of years, largely looking the same but growing ever brighter and shinier. I had planned to just sit here, have a couple of drinks and watch the normal goings-on unfold around me. But my initial plan of staying largely out of sight is starting to look like a bad idea.

ONE NIGHT STAND

From my corner by the window, in between sips of Baileys on ice, I keep eyeing him. Black jeans paired with sturdy biker boots and an untucked black shirt covering his broad frame on top. He looks like an imposing figure, even hunched over as he is at the bar. Like a giant.

I wish he'd turn around. I also wish I had bought my drink from this bar counter rather than the other one, at least I could have had a better look at him before finding my seat.

Like a reluctant predator, I'm just sitting here and staring at him from behind. If I hadn't chosen to sit in such a discreet location, it might have been the other way around.

My phone distracts, a message from Akhil, asking about the meeting and if we can talk. It can wait. I came here to forget about the irritating client with the project I couldn't refuse, not to talk about it. Stuffing the phone back into my handbag, I resume my earlier observations.

His friends are long gone by now, leaving an unoccupied stool beside him and my glass is getting empty quickly. Shall I? It feels so reassuring being unnoticed that I'm very reluctant to get up. I guess I'm just a coward when it comes down to making the first move, and my dark corner feels so safe.

He takes a big last sip from his glass and I panic. What if he's going to call it a night? If he leaves now

I'll forever wonder what could've been!

Before I know it my feet carry me towards the bar, while I absent-mindedly smooth down my business-like grey skirt and waistcoat combo. Despite the buzz of the drunken conversations that fills the space, the clicking of my heels on the wooden floorboards is almost as deafening as my heart pounding in my chest.

He turns towards me as soon as I reach and I'm frozen in place. Concentrating on continuing to breathe, I tuck my black wavy hair behind my ear and glance in his direction.

I take in his strong Nordic features, his full lips and steely blue eyes that stand in stark contrast against the dark brown of his hair and short beard. All I can manage is a shy smile before hurriedly looking away.

My instincts served me well, if I had stayed in my seat, I would've regretted it. I feel tiny standing next to him, which causes me to feel an even stronger attraction. And his eyes on me, I can almost feel them stabbing and probing.

His hands are huge as well, manly. I wonder how he'd touch me, if those hands could be gentle or if they only know how to be rough. There's no sign of a wedding ring: what a relief.

It has been decided, I want him at any cost.

"What can I get you, darling?" The bartender

interrupts my thoughts.

"Oh I'll have a Baileys, thanks." Taking a deep breath I turn towards my mark. "Would you like anything, while I'm buying already?"

Surprised, it takes him a few seconds to respond. Or perhaps he's as distracted by our eye contact as I am.

"Ice?" the bartender asks. I nod in response before resuming to look at the giant's face again.

The short interruption appears to have helped him get his thoughts in line too.

"Another Guinness," he tells the bartender.

His deep voice matches his impressive stature and makes my heart jump a few beats. I put a tenner down on the bar, hoping that the goose bumps on my arms aren't too obvious.

"Mind if I take this seat?" I say, "You're not holding it for anyone, are you?"

"Sure, go ahead."

While I get onto the stool, our drinks appear in front of us.

"Cheers." I'm trying my best to sound a lot more confident than I feel.

"Cheers." His voice elicits another wave of chills to wash over me.

I desperately try to think of something to say. Apparently my brain thinks it's funny to only feed me utter clichés. I take another sip while trying to come up with something a bit less moronic than 'come here often?'

"You're here on your own?" I finally ask. Still pretty stupid but I can't do any better right now.

"Came with two mates of mine from work. They'll be around here somewhere, on the pull probably," he responds.

"And you've stayed behind? How so, got a girlfriend?" I blurt out the question before I'm able to stop myself. Still, the information is pertinent.

He blinks at me a few times, eyebrows pulled together possibly in surprise at my question.

"No girlfriend. And I opted to stay here because frankly I can do without the inevitable rejection."

"Understandable, I find it quite nerve-wracking to approach people myself."

He seems off, I wonder if I'm making him uncomfortable. But if there ever was an appropriate time and place to ask strangers prying questions, it certainly would be here and now; Friday night in a busy London pub.

He shakes his head slowly before lifting his pint to his lips. I follow suit but can't help wondering what he's thinking.

"I don't see how you'd have that problem. I'm sure you get plenty of attention without even trying," he says finally, almost mumbling the words into his glass.

I look him right in the eyes and helplessly give in

to my urge to grin before answering.

"Perhaps the attention I tend to get without trying isn't the one I want."

We just stare at each other for what feels like ages. Neither of us seem in a hurry to look away. I leisurely let my mind wander, still curious what his hands might feel like against my skin. And those lips...

Objectively speaking, he looks like the sort of guy you'd avoid messing with if you can help it. I'm certain that when he walks down the street, people will instinctively part to make way. At the same time his mannerisms, his way of speaking have me convinced that behind the imposing facade, he's a really sweet guy. I wonder what makes me so sure, I don't even know him... yet.

"George, mate!" Two figures appear behind us, one giving him a supposedly jovial smack on his shoulder. The dark expression on his face tells me he's not overly pleased for the interruption.

"Lads..." he says.

"Made a friend, I see? What's your name, love?" The scrawny one who smacked George on the shoulder is leaning against him now and hungrily looking at me.

It doesn't help that he's had quite a bit more to drink than me and it's showing. Meanwhile, the other one is trying to get the bartender's attention.

"Lucy," I answer. My flight instinct becomes too

strong to ignore. "Excuse me for a minute, guys."

I steady myself against George's arm while slipping off the bar stool. The apologetic expression on his face is quite endearing. I let go of him and start walking towards the facilities.

Hopefully by the time I'm done wasting some time checking my make-up, George will be by himself again. I suppose I can't blame him for staying at the bar while at least the creepy one of his so-called friends will make a fool of himself in front of every woman in the pub.

CHAPTER TWO

The Ladies' toilet is empty when I walk in, though had there been a queue it would've been a good enough excuse to take my time coming back to the bar.

While smoothing down my hair with my fingers in front of the mirror, I can't help wondering why he hangs out with those guys. When they came up to us, I really got the impression he dislikes both of them. I lean in closer, wiping off tiny bits of eyeliner that have made their way outside my lash line.

I'm relieved to find a condom dispenser on the wall next to the sinks and load it up with all the coins I have. It's best to be prepared, just in case.

The door opens and two girls stagger in, giggling and supporting each other by the arm. I catch the closing door as they pass me and sneak up to the corner from where I get a view of the bar. It seems that the coast is now clear. I guess creepy man and sidekick wandered off looking for more potential victims.

Luckily my seat is still unoccupied, or perhaps George held it for me. I feel a tad less nervous walking up to him and the unmistakable beat of my boots on wood is now more rousing than intimidating.

"So, where were we..." I say.

Climbing back onto my stool, I lean on one elbow and face him. If this is me attempting to look laid back, I don't think it's working. With both feet dangling high above the floor like a toddler in a high chair, looking cool is an impossibility.

He looks over at me, the relief evident in his eyes.

"I'm sorry about that, especially Steve, he can be a bit of a knob at times."

"That's okay. Was it that obvious that I was running away?" My eyes are drawn to his lips, watching him reciprocate my smile.

"A bit, yeah, you had me worried for a bit that you weren't just avoiding him. Well, glad you came back anyway," he says.

"Of course I came back," I say, "just wanted to time it so I'd get you to myself again."

We're back to staring at each other. I wonder why he hasn't made a move, asked any personal questions. The way he's looking at me does suggest he is interested.

Finally I reach out for my glass which is still sitting there and start sliding it back and forth on the wooden counter causing the half-melted ice cubes in it to clink together.

"So, George... are you local?" I look up, catching

his gaze once more.

It doesn't seem like he ever looked away.

"Sort of, just came in for a few drinks after work before heading home. I live near Heathrow. You?"

"Not really, I live in Reading and I'm only in town for one night, a business trip of sorts." I pause, wondering if I should clarify.

"I booked a hotel to save me the late journey home. It's only a short walk from here actually."

"Alright," he says.

Really, that's all? Subtle hints don't appear to be enough to convey my intentions for tonight.

Between the exchanged looks, the small talk continues for a little while longer. George is a programmer apparently, such a coincidence we both work in IT.

I give him my card with my contact details, scribbling on it to add my mobile number, but resist the temptation to go into more detail. After all, I came in here to escape work, not discuss it.

He studies the card, fidgeting with it for a short while before looking back at me.

"How about you, seeing anyone?" he asks.

Finally.

"Not for a while, no." I smile at him, waiting for a reaction.

He is interested, it's written all over his face. But why is he still making me work for it?

Inside my chest a confusing combined feeling of relief and nerves has built up. The tension between us feels strong, almost too intimidating.

I bite my lip and look down, underneath his half open shirt I can just about see a black Tee with a familiar looking band logo printed across the front.

"Say..." I lean towards him and push one side of his shirt out of the way. Just being so close to him and nearly touching his chest with my fingertips is making my heart skip way too many beats at once.

"Blind Guardian? What a coincidence, I love them!" I exclaim, nearly breathless.

It's impossible for me to contain my excitement and so I ramble on about my favorite songs and asking about his. Must be the nerves talking. He doesn't say much at all beyond naming a few titles and remarking how brilliant they were live.

Clearly preoccupied with staring at my fingers which are still holding onto his shirt, he stops talking again. I'm equally lost for words.

Time seems to move in slow motion when his hand finds my wrist, and pulls me closer towards him. Our faces move closer together until he finally looks up at me again.

His eyes look almost black in the subdued light and we're now so near that I can feel his breath tickling my face. His scent is pleasant, like a rather masculine sort of cologne with a hint of beer mixed in. The effects of the few drinks I've had already are making it hard for me to focus but I know what I want, and I desperately hope he does too.

"You're making it very difficult for me to resist..." he says.

I see the same nerves I feel mirrored in his eyes momentarily. But instead of acting on them, he continues to stare deep into my soul.

"That was the idea..." I breathe.

Both of us are ready to go where our instincts might take us, still my mind plays tricks on me by announcing his idiot friends' return. I can hear the creepy one even if I don't know or care what he's saying. It's making me want to run and hide again, away from all interruptions.

He releases my wrist so I can I run both hands up his shoulders and around his neck. I hardly need to make any effort to get him to come closer, he already stood up right in front of me.

George is quite a bit taller than he looked sitting down. With me still perched on my bar stool and him standing, I can reach him perfectly. I run my fingers through his ponytail while our lips meet.

His arms find their way naturally around my back. The world around us disappears, taking any unwelcome other people away with it. My legs part as far as they'll go in this skirt to allow him closer. If his lips are anything to go by, he is the gentler type definitely. Or perhaps he just likes to start off that way.

Meanwhile I crave more than the teasing kisses he is planting on my lips, I tilt my head slightly. My arm is firmly wrapped around his neck now, my whole body completely giving in to his embrace. Encouraged, his lips part, as do mine. His beard feels ticklish against my face, an extra stimulus to drive me insane.

A jolt passes through me when our tongues meet. I thought I'd had butterflies in my stomach before, but nothing I've felt before could prepare me for what he's doing to me now. Hungrily I accept him into my mouth; caressing, licking and tasting him. The room is spinning around me but his arms keep me steady.

He pulls back only slightly, upon opening my eyes I see his, burning with lust.

"You taste divine," he whispers.

I rest my forehead against his and tug at his bottom lip with my teeth.

"Let's go..." I say.

CHAPTER THREE

Our moment of passion hasn't gone unnoticed, attracting quite a few stares. Ignoring his mates, who are just silently gawking at us, we stalk across the room towards the exit. Despite the substantial heels I'm wearing, he's still a good half foot taller than me.

The chill in the early spring air becomes more obvious as we rush across the street. His arm rests protectively around my shoulder and mine around his lower back. I feel like I'm on top of the world, like nothing could stop me from getting exactly what I want.

In the bright lights of the hotel lobby, I get a chance to admire our reflection in the polished elevator doors. The contrast between us is startling, it only turns me on more. The surrounding air feels warm but does nothing to subdue the goose bumps covering my entire body. I need him now, his touch, to make everything better. If only the lift doors would open...

After half an eternity, the bell chimes and doors jerk into action. We swiftly move into the lift and I'm aching to get my hands on him the moment we're alone and out of view. I press the button and wait. A quick look in his direction and sure enough, he's as focused on me, ready to continue our earlier affections.

The wicked smile on my lips vanishes when I see an elderly couple approach, rushing to make it into the lift before the doors shut. Especially the lady looks disapproving of us, dampening my spirit slightly. All I manage is to squeeze his hand on my shoulder and press against him closely to allow them to join us in the tiny space until we reach the third floor.

The pause between the ding and the doors opening lasts forever, I'm that impatient.

We escape and the grumpy couple is now out of sight. I turn towards him for more kisses while fumbling with the key card outside my room.

We barely make it inside before items of clothing start to come off.

I rush to unzip my boots, kicking them across the room, and unbutton my waistcoat. George has stepped behind me now, leaning down to kiss the back of my neck. After wriggling out of my waistcoat I throw it over the sofa against the wall and face him again

His eyes burn into me, lit up by what I can only assume is an intense hunger matching my own. He looks down at my cleavage, which is still more or less covered by my white blouse.

ONE NIGHT STAND

"Tell me I'm not dreaming," he says.

I start to unbutton from the top down.

"I should hope not."

He wraps his hands around my sides, digging his fingertips into my skin. Having fully opened my blouse, I move on to ridding him of his shirt, pushing it off his broad shoulders struggling to reach.

"Wow, you're tiny..."

His hands rest on my sides for a moment, then travel around to gently stroke my back. Indeed now that I'm no longer wearing heels he's towering over me even more.

"That may be so," I say, slipping two fingers into his belt and firmly pulling him against me, "but I'm not fragile, you can be rough."

But he isn't. Instead he lets his hands travel back down softly, cupping the fullest part of my butt. It doesn't take long for him to find the zipper of my skirt.

Feeling his soft belly pressed against me drives me wild and the promise contained within the harder, pointier bulge underneath makes my juices flow readily by now.

Our kisses have become wild and rushed, only interrupted by the odd moan and gasp for air. I let my fingers explore his skin underneath his t-shirt, running up his side, feeling every curve and ripple of flesh. I try my best not to claw at him, instead caressing the hair on his chest and stomach. He is all man and I can't wait to discover more of him.

As I start to lift his t-shirt upwards, he stops and holds my hands in place.

"Wait," he says.

"Why?"

He doesn't respond, making me wonder if I did something wrong. But these thoughts fade away with the overload of kisses he lavishes on me; behind my ear and trailing down my neck.

"Ohhh!" I shake and twitch and he continues to tickle me.

Overcome with desire, I dig my fingernails into his back. He doesn't seem to mind, if anything he pulls me towards him tighter.

I decide to let my hands roam once more, this time downwards. As soon as I slip my hand into his back pocket he suddenly pulls back. What have I done wrong?

The expression on his face doesn't give me any hint that he's uncomfortable, neither do his actions. He takes his time looking at me, slipping my blouse off my shoulders and stripping my skirt all the way down. I step out of it, thankful I went with bare legs today rather than unflattering pantyhose. He traces the outline of the black lacy thong with his fingertip.

"May I?" he asks, hooking his finger into the waistband, stretching it slightly.

ONE NIGHT STAND

"Please..." I say, watching him pulls down my knickers.

He takes a sharp breath while admiring the view.

Both hands on my hips, he falls to his knees in front of me. I'm taken by complete surprise. Rubbing my thighs with his hands, he kisses my lower abdomen softly, then around my hip bones, before settling himself down on the ground. His breath feels warm against my skin, softly teasing me.

A cry escapes my lips when I feel the first kiss. His fingers gently guiding my thighs apart, he moves in closer. Softly licking and teasing my clean-shaven skin, he makes me feel like a goddess. I tilt my hips to allow him better access and like a willing subject, he eagerly responds.

My hand grips tightly around his on my thigh. Our eyes meet and I just melt. Letting my other hand rest on his hair, I savor the moment. The flicking of his tongue against my clit causes jolts of pleasure to travel through my lower abdomen. How he skillfully changes style and licks me deeply at regular intervals is utter perfection.

"Enough, or I won't be able to last..." I breathe.

Immediately, he straightens himself and gets up. I reach for his face, drawing his lips into mine. I can taste myself on him. My interruption is quickly forgotten and his hands are back on me, unhooking my bra.

My hands meanwhile fumble with his belt buckle and then proceed to tug at his t-shirt again.

"Take this off for me," I say.

Barely able to look away from my now exposed breasts, he raises his eyebrows in response.

"I'm completely undressed and there you are, all covered up." I playfully put a hand on my cocked hip and grin at him.

"Unacceptable! Let me see you."

"Not much to see." He sounds reluctant.

"I'll be the judge of that." I take a step forward and slip my hand under his t-shirt, feeling his skin burn against my fingers. Soft, irresistible.

He closes his eyes and breathes in deeply under my touch. Focusing on his jeans again, I pull them down, revealing severely tented cotton boxers. While he steps out of them I quickly retrieve a condom from my handbag, before dropping the latter on the floor.

Who would've thought this impressive man would be so shy? I'm not going to let it discourage me. Something inside me tells me I must please him in any way I can, that's what I'm meant to do. Surely he'll come around once I show him just how much he turns me on.

Taking him by the hand, I walk over to the bed. At the edge, I turn to face him and slip one hand into his boxers. He starts to shiver when I wrap my fingers around his solid length. My other hand starts to pull his shorts down, to be discarded on the floor along with the rest of our stuff.

"Lie down... against these," I whisper.

I point at the plush pillows, yet still keep a firm grip on his cock. It's easy to get what you want when you've got someone's man parts in your hand.

His breathing has turned ragged and irregular, but he complies, eyeing me all the while. If he likes what he sees, I've no problem being on display. And I'm certain I'll get that t-shirt off him very shortly without any argument too.

I hand him the condom and kneel down on the bed, straddling his thigh. He fumbles about with it, his hands shaking slightly. Oh the anticipation is killing me!

Despite the distraction of me rubbing my moist sex against his leg, he somehow manages to put it on. Then I guide his hand down between my legs.

"You've made me so wet..." I spread, allowing his other thigh between mine too.

"Oh God!" he gasps as his fingers touch my lips.

I wasn't lying, they're nearly dripping. Moving up higher, I slowly tease him by rubbing myself against him. His balls and cock become slick with my juices and the direct contact gives me shivers.

He won't refuse me any longer.

Leaning down, I nibble on his neck, painfully aware of my tense nipples poking him in the chest.

My hands find the skin on his sides once more, but rather than linger there, I start peeling his t-shirt up.

His hips jerk upwards, betraying what he really wants.

"Only if you take this off for me," I whisper in his ear while tugging at the fabric which I've now managed to get halfway up his stomach.

Flutters of excitement rush through me, watching him lean up and fulfill my demand. He does not disappoint, soft skin with just the right amount of hair trailing down from his chest. Flawless, except for the half dozen or so scars on his right side and a very detailed tattoo covering his shoulder and part of his chest. Fiery dragons amongst intricate patterns of smoke, it's breathtaking.

I lean forward with both hands against his chest, lifting myself over him until the tip of his manhood presses up against me. I'm throbbing with anticipation, but won't allow this first move to be over too quickly.

My lips find his for a deep kiss, while I ease down slowly but surely, my hips into his until he has filled me completely. The moment is perfect, I wish it would linger.

We moan in unison when our bodies are joined.

"You feel amazing..." I say, grinding my hips into him deeply to underline my point.

Every forward movement causes my tummy to

press against his soft flesh and I love it.

His hands have a firm hold on my hips, guiding me into a faster rhythm. I run my fingers over his chest and kiss his neck and shoulders.

"Now I know I must be dreaming." His voice is strained, out of breath.

"I've never had a dream this good," I respond, equally breathless.

Bending down deeper, I let the tip of my tongue trail across his chest until I find his nipple. Sucking and licking it, watching him writhe beneath me.

I can't stop, wanting to push him further towards the inevitable. On knees and tiptoes I ride him harder and faster. His fingers dig into my flesh and his eyes shut. Ever since we first looked at each other, our lust has built up, begging to be released like this.

Despite the impersonal, slippery condom that separates us, I feel myself getting ready. A warm, gushing feeling is spreading through my insides, cheered on by the slight twitching of his cock.

He grunts with every push and squeezes my thighs. It's as if I can feel the pleasure building inside him, coursing through every vein and rearing to be freed. Sitting up straight on him now, I push harder and faster. I need to see his face, to know I made this happen. Lifting one of his hands off my leg, I push it up against my breast.

"I'm yours. Feel me!" I scream.

His eyes flick open and brows crinkle together and his other hand finds its way further back, grabbing my ass. He's ready and so am I, for the final push. I fuck him harder yet until he freezes and cries out something unintelligible. So very close myself, I enjoy the helpless look on his face and finish as well.

I collapse on top of him. Nothing left but a quivering mess, resting on his warm, inviting torso.

His arms wrap around me and there is nowhere I'd rather be.

I don't recall ever cuddling a stranger from a pub, but at this moment it feels right. The other unusual thing I'm noticing is that my desires have not been satisfied completely, despite the aftershocks of this intense orgasm still coursing through me. But I'm too tired to move, at least for now.

"I don't know what I did to deserve this..." he sighs.

CHAPTER FOUR

Snuggling deeper in his arms, I close my eyes and smile. Our moment of bliss doesn't last though, because I'm compelled to move by a sharp, sudden pain.

"Cramp! Let go!" I cry.

As soon as he releases me I manage to stretch out my aching muscles.

Much better, but I'm still feeling inexplicably clingy. Suddenly very nervous, I want his arms around me some more, but don't know if I could deal with refusal if the moment has already been ruined.

Rubbing the cramped part of my hip, I sit down and watch as he removes his condom and ties a knot in it. Carefully he places it on top of the empty wrapper on the bedside table.

My thigh is so close to his I can feel the warmth radiate off him. He's looking at me, as though he wants to say something but doesn't. Instead he lies back, his arm stretched out just far enough in my direction for it not to be coincidence.

I lie down as well, my head on his chest, relieved when he starts to hold me again. Although he appeared more relaxed only moments ago, he tenses up straight away when I rest my hand on him. I don't move, instead I listen to his heart racing underneath my ear. Gradually, he calms again, and I snuggle my face against him. He starts to caress my hair and shoulder.

"Mmm, that feels good," I whisper.

In a gesture that makes me feel so very special, he kisses my hair a few times.

No longer can I resist, and I let my fingertips roam over his body. Though his breathing turns irregular, he doesn't stop me and continues to do the same to me.

"This is some very nice artwork." I start tracing the outlines in his tattoo.

It's impossible to hold back on the one thing I know I shouldn't do: start an interrogation.

"Why so nervous earlier?"

He shrugs.

"Well don't be," I say.

Leaning up on my elbow, I kiss his chest where my head was resting until now. I'm finished exploring the patterns of his ink, and let my fingers run through his chest hair instead before heading down his side.

"What happened?" I ask, as my fingertips reach his scars.

"I used to work as a bouncer a few years ago. Ended up getting stabbed." His tone matches the length of his sentences. Clearly this isn't his favorite topic.

"I hope they got the guy," I whisper, before bending down and kissing every one of the five thin marks. He flinches at the first kiss but relaxes thereafter.

When I'm done, he pulls me back into his arms and starts playing with my hair. I respond by snuggling closer against him, one thigh over his, and caress his leg with my foot. Looking down, I'm pleased to find that he's still a bit hard.

"I haven't been with anyone since." His voice is a whisper, as if he's merely thinking out loud.

So that explains it. The lingering ticklishness in the pit of my stomach flares up again. In all likelihood I'll only have him for one night, but it should be one to remember for the both of us.

"In that case, one good turn deserves another," I chuckle, "And this time you're on top!"

Lifting my head, I grin at his bewildered expression and kiss his lips.

"No way, I'd crush you," he says finally.

"Try me," I dare, still grinning.

A glint appears in his eyes as he grins back at me. He grabs both my wrists and flips me off him and onto my back. Pinning both my wrists back onto the pillow, he leans over and just looks at me again. My eyes, lips and further down, before settling on my eyes again, there is a tenderness about him which I've not encountered before. He's something special.

"Let me know if it's too much..." he whispers.

I smile and shake my head.

"Kiss me some more!"

With both hands around his neck, I pull him into me. He lowers himself down until I'm sandwiched tightly between him and the mattress. Now that I'm finding myself in exactly the position I envisioned when I first laid eyes on him, I'm starting to feel feverish. Just one little detail is still off...

Reaching around, I carefully slip off the elastic holding his hair together allowing locks of brown hair to fall down framing his face.

"God yes, that's so hot!" Through the haze, I note that he's smiling again.

I'm not pretending, not wishing for something or someone else like what might happen during any other casual encounter. And it seems he has started to realize that I'm responding to him, not a dream or pretence.

Lost in further kisses, I'm cocooned between his strong arms either side of me. Both my hands roaming freely over his back, I can feel him starting to relax. I'm having a hard time pacing myself, having just found my favorite part of his anatomy.

Love handles.

How can something with such an enticing name be considered so undesirable? Running my fingertips over his sides softly at first, I can feel the goose bumps on his skin, though he does not say a word. Not too ticklish then, perhaps just a little.

But I want more, handfuls more!

As he finds a comfortable position on top of me, it is starkly obvious that not all about him is soft. I haven't touched his cock after getting off him the first time around, yet it is very prominently pressing against my thigh. I try to move underneath him but am unable until he lifts himself a bit, allowing me to spread.

I can think of nothing, but wanting him again and again. He leans on his knees between my legs, one hand resting to my left, the other reaching down. There is silence all around us, except our excited short breaths. All I can do is stare into his eyes, letting the anticipation build.

"Fuck," he interrupts and looks around to the night stand, "are there any more condoms?"

"Yes, my bag." I point to the floor.

He raises himself and stretches his arm to checks my handbag, retrieving several foil packets.

"Just in case," he grins. I like how he thinks.

Sat down on his knees between my spread legs again, he starts to put on the rubber. I lean up on my elbows, watching him. I try not to stare, for fear of making him uneasy but it's hard not to. Sure enough, he glances up at me through the strands of hair hanging in front of his face.

"Almost done."

I just smile in response and wait, trying not to be too impatient.

He seems in an equally big hurry, because he's back on top of me already, forcing my legs wide. With his hair loose and his eyes as passionate as I've ever seen on a man, he looks powerful. He enters me with new found energy and it's clear he has been completely transformed.

Gone is the shy IT guy whose character differed so much from his wild appearance. I'm being conquered by his inner Viking warrior. He plunges into me deeply and I cry out, squeezing my eyes shut involuntarily.

But I force myself to look again. I don't want to miss even a moment. Every movement of his, its sole purpose is seemingly to teach me that the tables are now turned. I had him where I wanted him when I was on top. Now it's his turn.

Helpless, legs wrapped around his thick waist. We must look like quite a pair, hair flying wildly around us, tickling my nose. I drag his face down towards me and feel my chin getting raw from the scratching of his beard. Still I demand more kisses.

And he's so good, so strong. I try to tell him, but it's all just coming out in strained fragmented sounds. The intense look in his eyes signals that he knows.

ONE NIGHT STAND

He fucks me harder and I feel my body reach new heights. Every muscle has a mind of its own, I spasm and contract and scream. But he keeps going and I've lost it.

When he thrusts into me finally, my cunt stings from the impact yet I'm fully satiated. Tears wet my face but I can't help smiling.

Little beads of sweat have formed on his brow and he looks down at me like he has just awoken from a dream. Carefully he lowers himself onto his elbows above me, just about managing to reach my streaked cheek with his fingers.

"Did I hurt you?"

"God, no," I say, "That was by far the best fuck I've ever had."

He takes a moment, scrutinizing my expression. If he's looking for a sign that I'm faking it, he's not going to get it.

Releasing him from the hold my legs had maintained on him, I allow myself to relax rather than risk another irritating cramp. He puts his head down on my chest, but is mindful not to weigh me down too much.

I'm grateful for the moment of rest and not in any hurry to let him go. And this time around it's me playing with his locks. Shame on whoever decided men should have short hair. They shouldn't.

This is what a man should look like. It's also how

one should fuck.

He lifts himself off me after a little while, seemingly as reluctant as I am. Once again I watch him and wait. The alarm clock next to the bed flips to 2:00 and I feel the long day catching up with me.

When he gets back into bed, he nudges me aside slightly and off the duvet. I have neither the will nor energy to move, and just wait while he pulls the covers over the both of us. With one big scooping movement of his arm, I'm drawn back.

His warm, reassuring presence surrounds me and I wouldn't change a thing about it. Not even the prickly hair of his still naked crotch pressed against my ass or the slight tickle on my neck caused by his every breath.

It has been a while since I slept with and not just fucked a man. The realization of how nice that kind of trust can be had been only a distant memory until now.

Relaxing utterly, for me there is no more fighting the inevitable.

CHAPTER FIVE

When I wake up, all is dark around us. I can hear his breathing next to me, deep and regular, but I'm completely restless. The night is ending and it hurts. It's not that I regret what happened, but I fear I may have gone about it all the wrong way.

This wasn't my first one night stand by far but it's certainly the first time I've felt this way after. Or during, for that matter. What's up with all this emotional crap?

My eyes are starting to adjust to the light, or lack thereof. The edge of the bed is starting to become visible, as well as the small couch at the far end of the spacious room which has some of our combined clothes piled over it.

Taking care not to wake him up, I lift up the sheets and slip out of bed. Suddenly I feel this incredible urge to cover up, to make myself just slightly less vulnerable. Luckily I had already laid out a nightie over the backrest of the couch, which I quickly put on.

Rummaging through my handbag, I locate my phone and earphones. Battery died, fucking great. I put it on charge but it'll some time to become usable again. Feeling in quite urgent need of some music, I decide to check his pockets for a more immediate solution.

I'm in luck, there's an iPod in his jeans and it has plenty of battery life left. Hope he doesn't mind, but then again I'll probably never see him again after today anyway.

iPod in hand, I shove our clothes towards one side and sit down with my legs folded. Going into his playlists, I find the most played songs and start to listen. I close my eyes and let the music wash over me, calming me down.

Since I opted for the most listened-to songs, I'm again reminded of how similar our tastes are. I feel like I'm getting a glimpse of his personality through music. It's with a lot of difficulty that I remain quiet instead of tapping or humming along with the faster numbers.

I try to make sense of my thoughts, as I am, isolated from reality and surrounded by guitars and drums. I wasn't drinking particularly much and I don't think anything got slipped into my drink. But last night felt different than a normal casual hook-up would have. I noticed him by the bar, so far so good. I approached him, and then everything changed. The moment we made eye contact it was like a switch inside my head was flipped.

No longer did I want an anonymous bit of fun, but

I wanted him. I wanted to know him, find out what makes him tick. Above all, I wanted to give him pleasure rather than fulfill my own needs.

I'm startled by a touch on my shoulder and open my eyes. Fuck, he's up. I look up at him briefly while turning off the iPod and handing it to him but can't bear to make eye contact.

"Sorry I borrowed this, hope you don't mind..." I say.

"No, not at all... Lucy...." he pauses.

"Yes?"

"Umm... I'm not sure how these things work, but I...."

I wish he'd just come out and say it. He wants to head home, obviously. Staring at the floor, I just wait for him to continue.

"Did you want me to leave? I mean, you were gone when I woke up, I thought perhaps I've made you uncomfortable by staying the night."

"Not on my account, stay as long as you like," I say, trying to not to sound as low as I feel. "I just couldn't sleep."

"How come?" he asks. "Hope I wasn't snoring!"

I let out a chuckle and look up at him. The concern on his face looks genuine, the situation would be quite comical if it wasn't for my confused emotional state.

"Don't worry, you weren't," I respond. "Actually, I

couldn't sleep because... I didn't want this to end."

He remains quiet for a few seconds, then he leans over and picks up all the clothes and dumps them on the bed. As he sits down beside me, the warm sensation of his thigh pressing against mine is putting me on edge.

"And you thought I did want it to end?" he asks finally.

"I don't know, isn't that how it usually goes?" I say.

"So let me know if I understand this correctly..." he says, "you want me to stay?"

"Yes." My voice is a whisper.

"And then?" he asks.

I just shake my head. Being honest is such a struggle.

Rather than putting myself out there, it would've been so much easier if I had told him to just leave initially. Less risky, because surely I'm just being a silly, needy cow right now. Every guy's worst nightmare after a perfectly good fuck the night before.

Tears are burning in my eyes, suddenly it feels like I have everything to lose.

"Why don't you first tell me what you want?" I whisper.

He takes my hand and strokes it with his fingers. It tickles just a little and waves of delicious goose bumps travel up my spine.

"More," he says.

I'm taken aback by his answer. All this is getting a bit weird, not at all what I expected to hear and I wonder if I just misunderstood him.

"What do you mean, more?"

"I want more than just one night with you. But I worry that I can't have that."

"What if that's exactly what I want too?" I ask, stealthily exploring his very serious expression from the corner of my eye.

"You hardly know anything about me. Don't make up your mind just yet."

"So tell me about you," I say.

"I don't want to pretend, it wouldn't work." He takes a deep breath before continuing.

"You could say I'm a bit of a loner, mostly by choice. But lately, I've found heading to the pub every night a lot easier than facing an empty house."

Despite how sad his admission is, I have to suppress a smile. We really are not so different; if there's one thing I can relate to it's loneliness.

"I've done that," I say. "Sometimes hooking up with someone, sometimes staying until closing."

Surely now he'll be the one to change his mind, even if my actions last night may have already suggested that this wasn't my first casual encounter. I dare not look up, not even when he wraps his fingers around mine tighter.

I feel the need to justify myself, to voice observations that only now are becoming apparent to me.

"But I've never asked someone to come back with me, not once put myself in a position where I couldn't just escape without a trace."

He sighs. I wish I knew exactly what he's thinking. It's a lot easier to say you want to be honest than to actually follow through.

In the silence that follows, my heart skips a few beats when he lets go and raises his hand. He guides my face upwards by my chin until I can't help but look at him.

"What made you approach me last night?" he asks.

There isn't a hint of humor in his eyes, no sign that he's only playing with me.

"Because I didn't think you would've, even if you had turned around at some point and noticed me looking at you... Was I wrong?"

"No, I guess I wouldn't have," he admits. "As it was, I barely knew what to do when you sat down next to me."

"I can't quite explain what happened. When I saw you, I just had to talk to you. Of course I hardly knew what to say."

"And I thought I was the awkward one." He smiles at me and caresses my cheek, making me forget just how tense I felt only seconds ago.

"And what makes you different from all the guys who are all too happy to get something quick and easy with no strings attached?" I ask. "Why want more?"

He pauses before answering, but does not take his eyes off me.

"The way you looked at me last night, actually the way you're still looking at me now... Like I'm someone worth seeing," he says. "That's a rare thing, something worth keeping and taking a risk on."

"You know, check out isn't until eleven..." I get up from the couch and take his hand again. "What do you say?"

"I'm sure we can find a way to pass the time."

CHAPTER SIX

When we get back into bed it feels somehow different. On one hand there is more riding on this now, with both of us putting ourselves in a vulnerable position. But I'm actually more comfortable. There is no rush, the morning deadline no longer applies.

Lying sideways, facing each other, he takes me into his arms.

I know now what he meant when he described how I looked at him. It's the same way he explores my face now, lingering on certain features just that little bit longer before coming back for eye contact. I feel noticed, appreciated.

It's a strange thing, when you look at someone's face after you've developed some kind of feelings for them. We can look at a model on a billboard and appreciate their attractiveness on an objective level, but eventually you'll get bored and look at something else.

But when you like someone, there is so much more to see. You won't lose interest even if you stare at them for hours. Perhaps it's knowing that you'll miss them when you're apart and you want to memorize their face to keep with you at all times.

ONE NIGHT STAND

A glint appears in his eyes and before I can wonder what he's thinking he firmly grabs both my wrists. He turns onto his back and I've no choice but to be dragged along.

"You interrupted me last night, it'll not happen again." His deep voice is not one to argue with.

He lets go of my hands and instead lifts me up from under my armpits. My legs spread, surrounding him, but he's not satisfied with me yet.

"Sit on me," he says.

"I already am..."

He shakes his head, dragging me upwards by hooking his hands through the bend of my knees. A smile forms on his lips when I begin to understand and crawl further upwards, finally ending up covering his face.

It wasn't the drink that made this so amazing the first time around. He does know exactly what to do, but more than that it's obvious he enjoys this as much as I do.

The moment his tongue reaches my clit I am positive that whatever happens between us, it'll be a fun ride. I'm taken over by waves of pleasure, starting small like a little itch scratched in just the right manner, then growing in intensity.

His strong hands keep me in place by my hips, even when I involuntarily try to twitch and wiggle. Now that he has me right where he wants me, there is no way he'll let me go before seeing this through.

I feel my stomach tighten, breaths become deeper and louder. Upon looking down I find that he's staring at me. His blue eyes shine unnaturally brightly in the dimmed light of the table lamp next to us. His beard is slightly raspy against my sensitive skin but it does not detract from the magic of the moment.

His tongue is surprisingly long, reaching quite deeply inside.

"Oh God, you're killing me," I moan.

Then, with furious flicking of his tongue I can't take it any longer. I am taken over, crying out for him. Falling back when he finally leaves his powerful hold on my hips, and sliding off to the side of him, I'm completely spent.

He gets up, admiring his work with a smile. I close my eyes and concentrate on getting my breathing back under control and the world back into focus.

A moment later I feel him next to me, his hand cupping my cheek.

"Lucy," he says.

I open my eyes to find him sitting beside me, my phone in hand.

"Someone's calling."

Such terrible timing. I lean up and read the name on the display. Akhil. Dammit.

"I should take this, I'm sorry. It's work." I sit up and pick up the call.

ONE NIGHT STAND

"Hello, Akhil."

His voice sounds excited, or agitated on the other end while he starts to ramble. It's not at all about the project but about him.

"Wait, what do you mean you're getting married and leaving?" I can't believe my ears.

He continues to tell me about his parents finding him a match, in good old traditional fashion. Now he's getting married to some girl he used to know when they were little, but whose family moved to Canada two decades ago. The preparations are well underway to make his immigration possible.

"Fuck... I mean congrats on the happy news... How come you're only telling me this now?" I rest my head in my remaining hand while listening to his apologetic explanation that he was nervous about letting me down. That's why he didn't say anything until he really couldn't put it off any longer.

"Alright well, all the best to you, and I wish you a happy marriage. Canada is nice, I think you'll like it there." I sound defeated; I feel it too.

Without being able to count on his support, I'll not only have trouble with this new project, I'll also have to rethink how I run my business in general. In a daze, I disconnect the call.

"That didn't sound good," George says.

I shake my head but I haven't got the words yet to explain it all.

"My project manager..." In a somewhat symbolic gesture I discard the phone on the bed.

"When I land a big project, he would handle the outsourcing side of things: manage people, ensure deadlines are met. You can't fucking trust anyone, can you. If only he had thought to give some notice!"

Deep breaths! I didn't have Akhil when I started out, it's not all going to unravel now that he's gone either. I hope.

"I guess I'll manage without him, it'll just be a lot more work..." I force a smile.

Not his problem but mine. I would happily move on from this topic of conversation sooner rather than later. But he is giving me a rather serious, thoughtful look. It's the sort of expression men get when they enter troubleshooting mode.

"How about finding a replacement?" he suggests.

I shrug. That won't be easy.

"You just let me know if there is anything I could do to help, alright?" he continues.

I smile at him again. It's a kind offer, but it would be wrong to ask that much of him. I'm not in a hurry to make this into a business relationship, what I want from him is a lot more intimate.

"Thanks, I'll keep it in mind. But I think it'll be OK if I handled the work myself for now."

He seems to have given up on the idea, instead lying down and gesturing at me to join him. Good plan, I could use some cheering up.

I start to look at him again, resting my head on his shoulder. It feels familiar already, like we've known each other longer than just a few hours. But feelings can be so deceptive, he's mostly a mystery to me.

"I want to know everything about you," I say.

"Are you sure?" He grins.

"Absolutely. Everything. For starters, what else do you like to do? Except frequenting old fashioned pubs and having great taste in music of course."

He seems a bit distracted but eventually does answer.

"I've got a motorcycle. A classic Harley."

A biker as well? This is great news and very fitting too. He completely looks the part for a Harley rider, I should've known.

"How exciting," I say, "perhaps we can go for a ride sometimes? Assuming it runs..."

He immediately notes my teasing tone and goes on the defensive.

"Oh don't tell me you're into that newfangled Japanese crap yourself? Just because it's an old Harley, doesn't mean it'll break down."

"Fair enough. Mine's Japanese yes, but also a classic. A 1970s Honda CB750 which might as well live at the local bike garage."

"You are full of surprises, aren't you," he says.

"I do my best."

He's beautiful, even if saying that out loud would just make things awkward. But there's no need to talk anymore. He leans forward, guiding my chin upwards to meet him. We kiss, slowly.

Every inch of my body has woken up to his presence again. As long as the rest of the world doesn't intrude, this moment between the two of us is perfect. A perfect beginning.

We talk more, kiss more, caress one another and look into each other's eyes. Like two blind people who just started seeing for the first time. Time passes with little relevance, until we are forced into action around ten-thirty. The night is truly over now.

He programs his number and address into my phone. Everything of mine is already on the card I gave him.

"This weekend I'm going to have to sort out the mess left behind by the guy, Akhil, who just quit. But I need to see you again. Soon," I say.

No response, he's quiet while putting on his clothes. Then he helps me gather my things from around the room.

"Maybe we can do dinner anyway? I'm assuming you'll still eat at some point while working," he says finally.

This is probably the wrong time to explain that I have a habit of forgetting all about meal breaks when I get sucked into work.

ONE NIGHT STAND

"Let's see, I'll call or text you when I see some light at the end of this tunnel." I zip up my overnight bag and see him observe me from across the bed.

Dressed in the same clothes as last night, his presence still makes me weak. I don't want to leave or say goodbye.

"Before we go, would you like to join me for breakfast?" I ask.

CHAPTER SEVEN

What a complete turd of a day. The whole weekend actually. I've stared at my screen without interruption throughout. Not even a meal break. This client might just become the death of me, especially since Akhil has run off to Canada without warning, and left me in this mess all by myself. It's hard to swallow my resentment at his betrayal.

I sit back, rubbing my eyes which have started to burn. No doubt I'll work late into the night again, best to take a break now and recharge.

Perhaps I should've said 'no' on Friday. Of course I couldn't know that I'd be stranded handling this shit storm on my own, but still. My instincts were telling me to run, and I should've listened! To hell with the money, I could've spent this time drumming up business elsewhere.

Some tea will help, maybe a sandwich too. The dull ache in my right wrist is another sign I need some time away from the computer. Otherwise it won't be long before the shooting pains start making their way up into my elbow.

I get up and wrap my bathrobe around me tightly. There's a chill in the air which I hadn't noticed earlier.

ONE NIGHT STAND

I didn't even realize how dark it has become, requiring me to switch on lights on my way downstairs to the kitchen. Until moments ago, I hadn't moved from my chair, not even looked out the window since this morning. I'm all stiff, tired, annoyed.

After getting home yesterday, the first thing I did was get rid of the uncomfortable business suit and throw on some pajamas, which I've been wearing ever since. The advantages of working from home are many, the disadvantage appears to be that it's easy to turn into a reclusive slob.

The second thing I did was switch off all those confusing thoughts that had muddled up my brain overnight on Friday. It hasn't even been forty-eight hours since I first laid eyes on George. But it took me quite a bit of effort to get rid of the thought of him. I almost managed it too.

Now that my focus has been broken, and I'm leaning against the kitchen counter, waiting for the kettle to boil, he's back though. As corny as it sounds, I do see him when I close my eyes. It's kind of nice as well as unwelcome. I don't have time for this.

A click tells me that the water is done, so I fill my mug, and watch almost in a trance how the contents turns progressively darker around the teabag in the centre. Swirls of brown escape through the fine paper mesh and spread throughout like writhing tentacles, until the color evens out. The spectacle brings back glimpses of memories from Friday night: George's hair, flying wildly while he was on top of me. His eyes, staring into mine, interested in *me,* as well as my body...

Lack of sleep must be getting to me.

Certainly on Friday there were more exciting things to do than sleep. And afterwards my own doubts and worries woke me way too early. Last night I went to bed at midnight but kept lying awake well beyond that.

Had Akhil not messed it all up, I may have had a moment to really absorb what happened on Friday. Instead it's one thing after another; needing to find a replacement, and reaching out to all the freelancers who normally answer to him to try to take over his role temporarily.

Plus I've had to make a start on the client's proposal.

Deep breaths. This isn't the first time I've been faced with a mountain of work and nobody to back me up. I'll be fine. I hope.

Goddammit, of all the times to have to deal with this sort of thing, the current timing is amazingly shit. If I mess up with this client, my reputation will most definitely take a battering. That's the sort of thing that's tough to recover from, with numerous competitors eager to take my place and the bank about ready to come knocking, should I miss my next repayment.

Every second geeky teenager is offering his web development skills on *Elance* at discount prices, so the industry isn't what it used to be. It takes a lot to survive nowadays.

Seeing the mug on the counter, still steaming, I am reminded to throw away the bag and realize I've left it in too long. Whatever, it'll have to do. The bread on the counter looks moldy, into the bin it goes. All I've got to eat right now is a pot of yoghurt from the fridge. Yoghurt and tea. Classy.

Right when I'm about to enjoy the first spoonful, I hear the familiar email ding on my phone. God, please let it be something other than further bad news. I try to finish eating first, but eventually cave and fish it out of the deep pocket of my robe. Apparently it's seven pm. Who would've known?

Dear Lucy , ... From George Townend? Who the hell is—oh crap, it's *George* George. It totally slipped my mind that I gave him my work email, and I never did find out his last name.

Seriously though? What man gets in touch right after a hook-up? Apparently George does. I'm not sure I can risk the distraction. Although part of me wants to close the email, leaving it for when I'll be more sociable, something makes me read on.

L. MOONE

Dear Lucy,

From what I could tell, the call you took yesterday morning shook you up quite a bit. I understand you'll need time to figure out how to deal with all that extra work now. Just to let you know, I was serious; if there's anything I can do to help...
Seeing as you're undoubtedly very busy right now, I didn't want to intrude, so I chose to email rather than call. I've been thinking about you, all day, and yesterday too.

There is no logical explanation for this, but the connection I felt with you is very real, special. This is new territory for me, I don't have the best of track records when it comes to relationships. All I know is, I do want more; I want to make this work. If I fuck up in some way (which I probably will, if the past is anything to go by), I hope you'll tell me and give me a chance to fix it.

You said you want to know everything about me; well I'm not sure there's that much to know. But maybe in a small way this email will help.

Music plays an important part in my life, how it allows for escapism in just about any situation. It was obvious—when I found you sitting with your eyes closed, lost in thought after having borrowed my iPod—that you function in the same way. Perhaps music is the best medium of communication for us and

ONE NIGHT STAND

I also hope this little soundtrack can help relieve some of the stress you must be feeling now.

I don't know if you listen to music while working, otherwise keep this for whenever you're taking a little break; I've put together a few songs that hold special meaning to me. Most of them have some kind of back story or they resonate with my moods at times, some I turn to again and again because they cheer me up. I'll let the music do the talking for now...

Hope to see you again soon,

George

There's a link to a <u>playlist on YouTube</u>[1] . Although I'm still skeptical, I decide to open it anyway and scroll through his selection. As much as I hate to admit it right now, he might be right. I need this.

I grab my tea and the half-eaten cup of yoghurt and head back to the office to find some tangled up earphones. My patience is wearing thin to the extent that I almost tear the buds off the wires trying to unravel them. Stupid, contrary pieces of shit that they are.

But then, the music fills me, not just my ears but all of me. In all my effort to get into business mode, I

---

[1] http://lmoone.com/fromgeorge

forgot this. I did a near perfect job of forgetting myself. With the tunes continuing on, I finish my food, sip the rest of my tea with my eyes closed, and am almost completely revitalized. Logic tells me the reason for that is mainly the sustenance, my heart tries to argue that it's the music and George's intentions behind sending me his selection.

When I'm done, I read his email again. And again. He thought of me all day. How sweet. He sent me this playlist to try to cheer me up; that's even sweeter. And to think that when his email came in just now, I actually felt annoyed about it. What the hell is wrong with me? It's no wonder I've been single for longer than I care to remember.

Right. After working my ass off for eleven hours, what's a few minutes to respond to him? It's actually nothing and I ought to be ashamed of myself for wanting to ignore him earlier.

Dear George,

Thanks so much for the email and the playlist. I've had a trying day and you seem to have shown up with impeccable timing to make it better.

Much like you, I also don't have the best history when it comes to relationships. Perhaps we can help each other in that respect. I can't promise much, except honesty.

ONE NIGHT STAND

Our night together feels like it happened so long ago already, and although I am absolutely swamped, I'm not sure it's healthy to go with my initial instinct of drowning in my work until the project is over. I'd like to see you again soon also. How about next weekend?

Lucy

I'm about ready to get stuck in again when my phone alerts me of his reply. I wonder if he's been waiting.

Dear Lucy,

I'm glad I was able to make a difference in a small way.

Next weekend would be great. How about we take our bikes out for a little ride, weather permitting? Lovely roads down near Winchester, perfect for a day trip. I can be at your place at 9:30.

And honesty is all I can ask for.

George

That does sound lovely, a day trip down south. I can't resist one last response, to mark the end of my break, telling him I'm looking forward to it. And I really am.

CHAPTER EIGHT

The week flew by. Long nights, early mornings, CV after CV finding its way into my inbox, and out again after being discarded. I should've known: Akhil is irreplaceable.

It took until Wednesday to realize that this project truly would land in my lap alone, and so I put my recruitment drive on the back burner in favor of pouring more blood, sweat and tears into Nightmare Client's proposal. It's been a steep learning curve, talking directly to the freelancers, all of whom seem to relish giving me vague answers no matter what question I send their way.

Last night the resulting proposal passed my final check and off it went, just in time for me to be able to enjoy my weekend with a full night's rest and no outstanding work on my To Do list come Saturday morning.

A glance through the curtains reveals that finally things seem to be going my way. This morning, the sun is streaming down and lighting up droplets of dew on my lawn. It's only eight, but there's not a cloud in sight.

By the time George gets here after breakfast, it'll

be simply perfect to head out for a lengthy ride. Contented and relaxed at last, I stretch the sleepiness out of my limbs one by one, only to be greeted by a nasty crack and one joint unable to free itself. This is a problem. A disaster, actually.

I hadn't been careful enough after the first warning signs popped up on Sunday: my right wrist has given up.

No way am I going to be able to ride for any length of time, with my accelerator hand out of action. Disappointment washes over me, but I refuse to be defeated just yet: I hope George's bike can carry two.

Juggling bike gear that has been sitting in the back of a closet for the best part of the winter, I head downstairs for much needed nourishment. Jeans should be sufficient for a spring day like today, especially if I'm riding pillion. Plus they look better than those big, all-weather trousers do.

The mug of tea feels heavy in my affected hand, it's uncomfortable enough for me to have to switch sides. No matter how often I stretch, flex and release my fingers, or attempt to rotate my wrist, it doesn't help. If anything, it's worse now than only moments ago when I first realized.

I decide to bandage it. And then I wait.

Checking the time, nine-twenty, I wait some more. By nine twenty-five, I'm unable to sit still anymore and pace about the kitchen, rearranging the odd cookbook here, and clearing away a stray breadcrumb on the counter.

And I wait.

At nine twenty-seven, I check my make-up in the shiny double-oven door. At nine twenty-seven-and-a-half, I brush my t-shirt down for what must be the tenth time, and force deep breaths.

This is ridiculous. I feel like a teenager waiting to be picked up for prom or something.

It occurs to me that I have about as much experience with dating as the average teenager. Perhaps less so. It's been a while... After spending the best part of my twenties building up my business leaving no time for socializing, once I hit thirty it seemed easier to just never allow anyone near enough to get to this stage. There have been a lot of lonely nights interspersed with the occasional stranger who never turned into anything more.

Weird, how these things happen. Little over a week ago, I couldn't have guessed I would find myself waiting for an actual second date, after picking up some guy who I initially only noticed from behind.

And yet...

He *is* going to turn up though, isn't he?

We've been emailing each other in the evenings, with him usually being a lot more prompt in his responses than me, suggesting he's still keen. But still, it's hard to ignore the niggling doubts that make their way into my overworked mind.

The bell rings, making me almost drop the cup I've decided to wash. *Shit, shit, shit!* He's here!

I rush to the door, nearly stumbling over my own feet in the process, take a deep breath and press the button on the security system.

"Hi!" My heart is hammering in my chest and I'm breathless and faint. If this is what I'm going to be like before he even enters the house, how is the rest of the day going to go?

On the small black & white video screen, a leather-clad George is shuffling about uncomfortably before leaning forward towards the microphone again.

"Hey, Lucy?"

Shit, the gate is still closed. I press the button and the two large metal doors swing into action, allowing him space to enter.

"Please come in, park up anywhere and I'll be right out."

He hesitates a moment, then returns to his bike, just off screen, and the vaguely familiar rumble of an old V-twin engine filters through my windows. He's coming in.

I head outside, and greet him with an awkward smile. He responds, with an equal amount of awkwardness, reluctantly eyeing the driveway, with the heavy security gates slowly moving back into place, the carefully manicured lawn that leads around the side of the house, the gravel paths, shrubs, the garage and finally the Victorian style villa behind me.

"Nice house."

"Thanks." I shift from one foot to the other, and try to decide on my next move while he puts his Harley on its side stand on the block paved, broad drive.

The bike fits him. It's like a throwback to another era, unmistakable 70s style wide handles and a bright orange paint job with black pin-striping to match.

"Lovely machine," I say, noting with relief that it indeed has space for two.

We look at each other for a moment, not quite sure what to do. The time apart has made things a bit weird, despite keeping in touch this past week. I swallow my nerves and approach him to give him a hug. He's even taller than I recall, requiring me to tiptoe to reach.

I'm not wearing heels today, of course! That explains it.

It's such a relief, having his arms close around me. The effect seems to not be lost on him either because after a deep sighs, he draws me against him tighter. The cool leather of his jacket against my fingertips gives me goose bumps, yet I don't really feel like letting go. I do release him anyway though, before things get even weirder.

ONE NIGHT STAND

"I almost thought I'd come to the wrong place. Not quite what I expected." The deep bass of his voice makes the hairs on my arms stand up.

"It's..." I shrug, looking for the right words. "Well, it's home, whatever it is."

I can imagine it's a bit of a shock, for someone living in the city to be faced with a house of this scale. But at no point in the past week would it have been appropriate to tell him I live in what is practically a country mansion compared to most city dwellings.

Is that something people do? Compare pay checks and lifestyles at the very beginning of getting together? I don't really know, it's all new territory to me and the topic simply didn't come up.

"Let's go in. Would you like some tea or coffee?" Shockingly, I don't even know how he prefers to take his caffeine. Guess I'll soon find out.

"Yeah, tea would be great. No sugar."

"Cool. That's how I have it too." I shoot him a smile.

Perhaps it's just that initial touch which soothed my frazzled nerves, but things are surely going to be easier now. *Aren't they?*

We head inside, with him about a step behind me all the way, no doubt looking around some more. I'd never really thought about how my circumstances differ from others my age. Obviously I realize most people don't live in a freestanding house in the countryside, but I still find it hard to imagine what his place might be like. Hopefully I'll get to see it soon enough.

While I put the kettle on, I try to grab the second stool from the other side of the breakfast bar and immediately regret it.

"Ouch," I curse under my breath, rubbing my bandaged wrist.

"Need a hand?" George steps towards me and effortlessly moves the stool I just struggled with. "What happened?"

"I guess I'm a bit overworked." I continue rubbing my wrist and try to stretch my fingers just a bit. Pointless, it's locked.

"Right. Believe me, it pays to take care of ergonomics when you're stuck at the PC all day."

I smile bitterly, knowing he's right. Unfortunately all good intentions have a funny habit of flying out the window when you get fucked over by your most important team member at the start of a crucial project.

"Here, let me." He picks up the kettle, which has just boiled, and pours the steaming water into the two cups I'd already lined up on the counter.

"It only just started this morning, but I didn't want to cancel. I'd been looking forward to our little outing all week," I say, clambering up onto the stool nearest to me.

He nods, still looking down at the cups, adding splashes of milk and waiting for the color to turn right.

"Well, you're not riding your bike today, that's for sure."

"I was rather hoping I could ride with you. If that's OK." I accept the cup he offers me with both hands, enjoying the brush of his fingers as they slip out from around the mug.

"Certainly. If you're sure you're up for it." He sits down with his cup beside me.

"I wouldn't miss it for the world." We share a smile, before having our first sips of the relaxing hot liquid. His eyes somehow speak to me more clearly than any words could. We're good. Today is going to be just perfect.

CHAPTER NINE

There's something special about being on the back of a powerful machine, which effortlessly manages to zip along the narrow winding roads of the English countryside despite its size. More so, when it's operated by an equally powerful man, whom I trust despite not knowing him well at all.

My safety, my life is in his hands in a way. When he accelerates, I have no choice but to speed up along with him. If he misjudges a turn, we'll both go down together. And yet, I couldn't feel more safe than I do now, on the back of George's bike.

The spring sunshine has lit up the surrounding fields, their slight damp glistening in the morning light. It's an absolutely gorgeous day, featuring crisp, cool air which I know will warm up later. We're well prepared so we don't notice the chill.

After driving for about an hour, we're nearing Winchester, a name more famous for guns than the natural beauty we're enjoying today. He's keeping off the busy roads, preferring the smaller, country lanes where thankfully you still do get the chance to go at a decent clip.

"Almost there," George remarks when we slow for

a particularly tight turn.

I smile, and wrap my arms around him tighter. If only I didn't have to wear this helmet, I could get even more comfortable behind him. Anyway, I'm determined to ensure I get that chance later today.

He pulls into a parking lot with only one other vehicle in it, the broad tires of the bike crush the dirty gravelly surface, making a distinctive crunching noise and we come to a standstill. We've arrived. The lot is adorned with the usual warnings and rules that apply to most nature reserves. Don't litter, dogs must be leashed, etc.

I initially didn't have much of an idea where we were going or what we would do there, but George had come prepared. His bike is outfitted with a pair of old fashioned leather saddlebags, which contain all the trappings needed for a good picnic. All I had to contribute was a thermos with yet more tea. It really is convenient that we take it the same way and the optimist in me wants to read some deeper meaning into that fact.

After locking up both our helmets to the sissy bar of the bike, he picks up most of the stuff, only permitting me to carry the picnic blanket with my good hand. Off we go, up the winding path through the hedgerows with all our supplies in tow.

"What a beautiful place," I remark, noting the gently sloping hills that surround the vantage point we're heading towards.

"Yeah, I love this area. But it's always a bit weird exploring these types of places on your own. People tend to look at you like you're a pervert if you go walking in the woods by yourself."

I giggle.

"I can imagine. Well, no such problem today."

"Nope. A perfectly wholesome day out and I've got the company to prove it." He turns to smile at me, then continues to climb the path ahead.

Once we reach the top of the little hillock and find a quiet corner in the sun, away from the breeze, I spread the blanket on the grass, allowing us to sit down. The sun has gained quite a bit of warmth, so we both take off our jackets to make the most of it.

George kneels beside me and unpacks various containers and wrapped parcels. I hadn't had time to realize how hungry I am, but as soon as the first items start coming out of their packaging, my stomach starts to growl.

"So, we've got some sandwiches, tea, obviously, various cold meats and cheese and of course, something sweet for after." He looks up from the spread he's laid out on the checkered blanket between us, somewhat shyly.

"Nothing too fancy..." he quickly adds.

"Looks perfect to me," I grin at him, grateful for what looks like an extreme amount of food for only two people. After the week I've had, I could eat a horse.

He hands me a paper plate and I'm having trouble deciding what to dive into first so I just take a little bit of everything when I note he's still observing me.

"Hungry?"

"Famished." I put the plate down in front of me and pour us some tea into the small metal cups that detach from the thermos.

"I was concerned, you know, that it wouldn't quite match up to your usual fare after seeing where you live." He brushes some strands of hair off his face, which had come loose from his ponytail, while taking off his helmet. Clearly he's not past the earlier awkwardness, he's still weirded out by what he perceives my lifestyle to be.

"It's not all foie gras and champagne, you know. I've been surviving largely on baked beans on toast for the past week." I don't add that with the way things have been going, I couldn't afford either champagne or foie gras anyway.

"Well then, I perhaps shouldn't have worried."

I raise my cup at him. "Cheers."

He responds with a similar gesture and we grin at each other for a moment.

I pick up my plate again, ready to take a big bite out of one of the sandwiches, but get distracted by the beautiful view. Pretty countryside as far as the eye can see, even the road and parking are hidden behind shrubbery, making it seem like we're in a different world. One without traffic jams, demanding jobs, and money worries.

His choice of destination is spot on. As are his efforts with the food. How incredibly sweet, a picnic for a second date. It certainly is quite the change from our first, which was a lot more one night stand than date. Who could've guessed that we'd end up here? It's only been a week, and I don't know the guy sitting opposite me. Not really, anyway. But I will.

"What's funny?" George asks, making me realize I've been sitting here smiling to myself like a doofus for much too long.

"Oh, I'm just happy to be here. With you."

He offers me another sandwich, which I gladly accept.

"These are great, by the way." I take another bite. "I'm impressed."

"That was the idea. Plus I didn't have any clue what people generally do on a date."

"Same here."

"Refill?" he asks, gesturing at my empty cup.

I raise it towards him, allowing him to pour. He steadies my cup with his fingers brushing past mine, putting me on edge again. *This.* This is what I want.

"It's weird," George remarks while letting go of me and the cup, seemingly reluctantly.

"What is?"

"Just, meeting up again. New territory."

He looks away, focusing instead on the vistas stretched out before us. I understand completely, and he totally spoke my mind too.

"Soon enough, it'll be old and familiar," I joke.

He lets out a laugh, and turns in my direction again.

I lean forward, suppressing a wince when I accidentally put weight on my sore wrist. This occupational injury is really cramping my style. He reaches out for me, cupping my face in his hand, which I gratefully lean into.

"You're still into it though, aren't you?" he whispers.

"Absolutely. I've been thinking about you a lot this week." I smile, enjoying the slight shiver that travels my spine when I allow myself to really look at him.

He leans in, pausing just before our lips meet, making me impatient. But he continues to take his time, staring into my eyes, as if asking for permission to continue. I reach for him, wrapping my arm around his shoulder.

It was always going to be a bit of a risk, seeing someone again when the first connection only occurred a couple of drinks into a night out at the pub. Of course things will start off a bit weird, it's only natural.

I pull myself closer against him, and find myself supported by his arm, drawing me in tighter. Our lips touch, and I'm blown away again by the softness of his kisses. He is a paradox, the ultimate proof that appearances can deceive.

His gentle nature only makes me like him better. Plus I know there's raw passion in there, which only takes a bit of coaxing to come out.

He lowers me onto the plaid blanket, and follows, his other arm surrounding me as well. The kisses continue, sending my heartbeat into a frenzy. He tastes amazing, and his scent... It is only now that I realize how much I love the smell of leather on a man.

I wrap both arms around his neck and cling onto him. In the background, various food containers clang together, as we try to make sufficient space for us. Soft, careful kisses are replaced by deeper, more desperate ones. He sets me alight, making me forget any lingering professional worries, any concerns about how to make this connection last despite any as yet undiscovered differences between us.

"I'm really glad I gathered the nerve to talk to you on Friday," I whisper into his lips.

"Me too."

He pulls back, looking at my face again, before brushing the odd lock of hair out of the way and behind my ear.

"And I'm glad I emailed you, despite wondering if that one night together was just a fluke."

"It wasn't, was it? I still feel the same."

He flashes a quick grin, and answers with further kisses, behind my ear, down the side of my neck, before pushing aside the neckline of my t-shirt enough to reach my collarbone.

My eyes shut involuntarily, that's how intense the butterflies in my stomach are. I'm in quite a state, confused whether I'm still a bit nervous, or just overcome by the chemistry between us.

"Your wholesome day out is taking an unforeseen turn," I remark, in an attempt to cut the tension, while still refusing to let go of him. I need more kisses, more affection, more of a connection.

"Who says this is unwholesome, or unforeseen?" he says.

In an incredible moment of déjà vu, my phone rings just as he starts to lavish the rest of my body with affections. I want to ignore it, but nobody ever calls me, except for my folks every other Sunday, or clients...

"You should probably get that," George whispers in my ear before releasing me.

"I don't want to," I respond, but I know he's right.

CHAPTER TEN

"Hello?" After recognizing the name on the display as the Nightmare Client, the tension I had managed to shed in the run up to today is back in full force. I had submitted the proposal on time and in full, what could he possibly want now, late morning on a Saturday?

"Thanks for sending over your estimate." Jack—Mr. Nightmare—Cleary manages to sound stern and humorless even through the phone.

"No problem, I trust it answered any lingering questions you may have had?" Despite my earlier disbelief, it seems we are really doing the follow-up now. This man has clearly never heard of work-life balance.

"Indeed, I'm about ready to move forward," Jack says, however his tone is inconclusive.

"That's wonderful."

George gives me a questioning look, clearly my own tone does not match my words either.

"But, before I'm ready to commit to such a big job, I'm going to need further reassurances that you and your team can handle the workload. Also, due to some other developments, my schedule for the new restaurant chain has moved up a bit, meaning I'll need the websites done sooner than the previously agreed date."

Bollocks . I suppress a groan. Of course he wants to change the parameters of the project now, that's so typical.

"I completely understand. If you could inform me of the revised schedule in writing, I'll amend my proposal as necessary."

"Fair enough. And in the meantime, I think the importance of this project justifies another meeting to sign the contract in person, this time I'd like to meet your team as well. I need to know everyone is on the same page and equally motivated to make this a success. I'll be in touch with potential dates."

My team? It's an open secret that most successful web design businesses nowadays outsource a lot of their work overseas. Local talent is hard to find at competitive rates. Of course it's a fine balancing act, having an overseas workforce, while not coming across as an unprofessional one-man, or in this case, one-woman band.

Naturally in my efforts to secure the project, I had followed standard procedure and not laid out the finer points of my operation with him. It's just not done.

"Meet my team? Well, I'll see what I can do."

"I'm glad we understand each other. Good day."

And again, as I put down the phone, I find myself in another pickle. I should've known, nothing about this client is simple and straightforward.

"More trouble?" George asks finally, while I'm rubbing my temples, trying to focus on next steps.

"I'm going to have to pull out," I admit, after letting the swirling thoughts in my mind settle. It's the only logical thing I can do. And then, if I don't land another project pretty much immediately, I will be in deep financial shit. The job I was trying to use to pull myself out of this mess, might push me further into it.

"What's the problem, he wants another meeting?" George asks.

"Yeah, with my *team*."

"He doesn't know you farm out the work."

"Well, ordinarily I could have always arranged a video conference with Akhil. He's always been good at putting clients' minds at ease, even remotely. Obviously, that's no longer an option, and this guy is never going to move forward if it's just me. I recognize his type."

George leans over again, and wraps his arm around me, pulling me into his lap. I close my eyes, and try to focus on his soothing touch, but it's hopeless. I can't relax right now, not while I'm faced with the potential loss of my carefully built up professional reputation, as well as financial ruin.

"There may be another way out," George says.

ONE NIGHT STAND

I look up at him, unable to wipe the skeptical frown off my face.

"Only if you're comfortable, but if you'll allow me to help... I do have project management experience."

Surely I can't take him up on that? He offered pretty much immediately when the whole Akhil situation went down, but what guarantee do I have that he's suitable for the role? I barely know him.

"I imagine you'd be busy enough with your own work?"

He shrugs, and looks away.

"Don't you worry about that. I can make time."

I'm still unconvinced, although if he were to at least take on the role of Project Manager temporarily, it would solve a whole host of issues. Worst case scenario, I replenish the coffers, best case, Nightmare Client will bring in follow-up business. If George is good at his work, that is.

And the freelancers, my God, if only they accept him.

He looks down at me again, and rests his hand on my shoulder. If he really is happy to help out, it would give us a lot of time together, getting to know one another...

I really need to think about this. I don't know enough about his experience or skills to make an informed decision. Although, the way he talks does suggest he knows his stuff.

"Look, I get it. We've only just met. I don't expect you to entrust me with your business just because some guy with the worst timing ever went and let you down. Think about it. Believe me, I really just want to help."

"I know. It's just... weird, and sudden."

He smiles down at me and runs his thumb over my lower lip as if he can't wait to taste me again. The gesture as well as the look on his face make me want to throw all caution in the wind. I want to trust him, take his hand and jump in the deep end together, no matter what the consequences. But I've poured ten years of my life into this venture, and I'll be damned if I'm going to risk all now.

"How about, we just spend the rest of the day as if none of this has happened?" I suggest, severely distracted by his touch. I'll think about how to resolve the Nightmare Client situation when I get home. There's no point making rash decisions in the heat of the moment.

"Sounds like a plan."

I slip off his lap and back onto the blanket, beckoning at him to join me on top again.

"Where were we?" I ask, only to be muffled when our lips connect once more.

I wrap my arms around him, as we're overcome by a renewed hunger for one another. Although this isn't the first time by far that I've been with a man, it is the first time I've felt such a need for another human being. Something tells me that's a first for him too.

That's got to mean something, right? Perhaps I can consider the idea of accepting his help. Just this once...

I run my hands up his back, exploring the contours of his shoulder blades. I love how my arms struggle to reach all the way around him, how he is so much taller than me, yet the gentle nibbles of his lips on my earlobe remind me that he'd never hurt me, at least physically.

How far can we go, in this relatively public place?

"I want you." The words escape me before better sense prevails and I can censor myself. It's true though.

"Then I'd better not argue," he says.

This time, we're not disturbed by a phone call.

This time, we're able to rekindle that passion which first surfaced last week Friday, and find that if anything, our desires are stronger than that first time even. At least mine are.

Although we do our best to keep things PG-13, just in case the odd fellow day tripper stumbles across us, I know today is going to be etched in my memory for a long time to come, hopefully forever. Picnics aren't just for family outings. They can be as romantic and sexy as anything, with the right company.

We spend the afternoon cuddled together soaking

up the rays on that checkered blanket in the grass, until the incoming clouds signal it's time to move. After a thrilling ride through the same quaint country lanes, he drops me at my place well in time before dark. Neither of us want to say goodbye just yet, but I have no choice.

It's time to start work on Nightmare Proposal 2.0.

I lean closer to my monitor in disbelief. April 25th? Nightmare Client wants the project done, and live, by April 25th? That's only about... I flip over the page on my desktop calendar and count the weeks. Five-and-a-bit. Jesus Christ. And he suggests we meet on Tuesday.

With the way things have been going, I couldn't even get the developers to commit to an eight-week timeline, reducing it down to five is just crazy talk. I take a deep breath and open up a new email screen to give him a piece of my mind.

Dear Mr. Cleary,

I regret to inform you...

Pfft, this isn't going to be easy. He won't be happy, and neither am I. It's only seven o'clock, and since the man seems to not have any social life, I'm pretty sure he will phone me up to express his displeasure as soon as I hit *send* on this.

Before writing anything further, I pause, head in hands, and try to really think. The fifty per cent advance on this would really come in handy, fifty per cent more upon completion even more so. But he won't buy in if I mess up the meeting; I'm sure someone else has got a bid in too.

While I'm still deciding what to do, my inbox flashes in bold to alert me of a new email. I may as well check what it is.

The subject line, 'Restaurant project' instantly grabs my attention. But it's not from Nightmare Client, but instead a vaguely familiar other name: Callum Byrne. I could bet that I've heard this name somewhere, but I can't place him.

Dear Ms. Aldwell,

A dear friend of mine, Jack Cleary, has referred me to you for an upcoming project. Much like him, I'm also planning to launch a new chain of gourmet restaurants, to coincide with the new season of my show on Good Food TV — Fuck, so that's where I've heard that name before!

I sink back into my chair, reading the rest of the email. A project similar to the current one, only this guy seems a lot more sensible in his approach as well as timescale. A lot of the custom programming that would be required right now could be reused, and his tone, as well as specific requirements suggest he's not the micro-managing type, which is good. And the suggested budget... It would take the pressure off for months.

I knew Nightmare Client's project would be prestigious, and open up a whole new market to tap into, but I hadn't expected him to send other business my way without finalizing our contract!

Flipping back to the email in progress, I suddenly feel stuck. If I argue too much, or worse, withdraw my bid, I'll no doubt lose this new project as well. But Jack's phone call earlier today had made it painfully clear that I can't succeed on my own either. Enter George, who is so eager to help out and appears to be qualified as well.

Both these projects are a massive deal, big enough to warrant taking a risk. Once I've got the first one done, I'll be home safe with the bank. And who knows how many other people Cleary, as well as Byrne, could refer.

I decide to discard my half-written email to Jack Cleary and instead pick up my mobile to dial George's number. Let's see what he says when I explain how big this opportunity is for me.

CHAPTER ELEVEN

I've been careful, evaluated the situation and his qualifications like I would've done with anyone else. At least on paper, George is the perfect candidate. Still, I'm having trouble trusting someone else, when Akhil's betrayal still stings so sharply.

Looking over at him sitting at the spare PC, concentrating hard on whatever's on screen, I try to justify my actions further and swallow my apprehension. He seems dependable, and truly motivated. Fingers crossed this goes well, and I haven't made a massive mistake.

How many people would have been happy to come here on a Sunday morning, to potentially work through the day and into the evening, preparing for a presentation that isn't even their job, technically? Nobody would have, yet here he is. True, I did offer him compensation above industry standard, but that's hardly the point. He didn't even seem to be listening when I mentioned the money.

"So we're shooting for a four week development time, plus 1 week troubleshooting and testing?" George asks, looking up from the revised proposal I'd just shared with him.

"That's right. And we've got to have our ducks in a row within the next two days, and present it to the client."

It's a very tight schedule, considering the amount of custom programming required to make his restaurant website one of the most cutting-edge in the industry. Cleary needs a fully integrated booking system of course, and a shiny user interface for customers and staff alike. This isn't just a matter of sticking a standard table reservation software in there. If that's what he wanted, he could've hired any old hack.

"It's ambitious, but not impossible. What system do you use to manage the development team?"

"Akhil used to be in charge of that, and he just sort of handled it all by email and Skype."

"Right. No problem." George scratches his beard, looking a bit unimpressed.

"How about I introduce you to the main players?" I suggest.

He nods and I get right to work, sending out emails to the senior freelancers. It had been a massive oversight on my part to give Akhil so much autonomy as project manager. Frankly, I don't really know how he managed everyone one-to-one while still having the time to report back to me.

I'd grown accustomed to instant and accurate responses, despite the time-difference between India and here. Yet when I tried to take over last week, it felt like I was getting bullshitted at every turn. It just hadn't worked quite the same. And now I've thrown George into this shit as well. Great. He's so going to hate me for this.

Glancing over again, I see he has logged on to Skype and is furiously typing away at something. I recognize the profile image in the chat window as one of the main programmers, Neeraj, who has been working for me for the past three years. Best to leave them to it, get to know one another.

"I'll make us some tea," I say, and George nods in approval.

On my way down the stairs, I can't shake the realization how strange this is, having another person in my office, which has often served as my refuge from the real world. I'm even wearing proper outside clothes today, rather than pajamas. It's making me anxious, handing over so much responsibility to another person again, right after being let down.

Once in the kitchen, I switch on the kettle and wait. We've got only a couple of days to figure out how this set up is going to work, and to present a united front with Nightmare Client. And all the while, I'm wavering between being grateful that George is here with me, and worried that things are going to go terribly wrong.

While I wait, I try to do a few simple hand

exercises, in an attempt to free up my wrist. Bandages, joint rub and a bit of heat managed to improve it overnight, but as soon as I sat down in front of my workstation this morning, I got a painful reminder that I wouldn't be able to work at full capacity for a while at least.

Thankfully now that the proposal has been finished, my workload is slightly reduced until we get into the user interface design stage. Those are the two things I'm good at: drumming up business, and making things look good. But all the glue in between is going to be down to the guys in India and George. This truly is a team effort, and I feel helpless.

I lay out a tray, and a packet of biscuits, before adding the two mugs and heading back up.

"So, we should be fine as far as time is concerned," George announces as soon as I re-enter the office.

"Really?"

"Yeah, I had a good talk with Neeraj, and we managed to prepare a rough timeline. Here, take a look." George pulls my chair up next to him and points at the spreadsheet on his screen.

I'm speechless. After trying my best last week to get a feel for the time they'd need to finish off their part of the development process, I thought it impossible to get a straight answer out of any of them. I kept wondering if they were just telling me what I wanted to hear without really committing to anything.

"How did you manage that? And in what - five minutes?"

George smiles knowingly. "Programmers know how to talk to programmers. I also suggest that you implement some kind of project management system, like Basecamp. It would help keep everyone on track."

He gets up just enough to reach the tea and cookies I'd forgotten on the desk.

"I don't believe it."

George hands me my cup, and I continue to stare at him in disbelief. Five minutes, and things are starting to come together.

"See, you've got to understand how these guys work. It's a cultural thing. There's a hierarchy to follow," George explains, before taking a sip.

"U-huh," I respond, but am not fully convinced yet.

"Tell the guy in charge what you want, and he'll say whether or not it's possible. Simple as. If you talk to the wrong person, someone lower down, he won't know what to say without running it past the senior guy first."

While George goes through the plan they've come up with, and shows me various bits of the spreadsheet they've done to organize it all, things fall into place. As he continues to explain, I start to feel relieved, mostly. By the end, I'm more optimistic about the project than I've ever been, and yet...

It's all going to work out, no thanks to me.

***

We sit back in the plush armchairs in my lounge, tired but at least I no longer feel like my world is about to implode. Today, with George's help the project has actually turned viable.

"Cheers," I say, holding up my glass of beer.

"To a job well begun," he responds, repeating my gesture.

Looking at him now, after having spent all day working together, my initial jealousy at how easily he managed to sort out my freelancer problem has waned. Fine, I may not be brilliant at handling staff, but at least I've got help now.

And it strikes me again that said help is absolutely gorgeous. We've been in work mode all day, focused on the task at hand, but now we're off the clock and the relaxed mood is shifting my attention.

"I just wanted to thank you again for all you're doing for me. Things may just work out." I put down my glass on the teak wood side table between us.

"Not a problem, it's an interesting project. A bit different from the usual." He smiles at me, then looks around the half-lit room, until his eyes are invariably drawn to the large flat screen TV on the wall at the far end of the space. "That's... wow."

I follow his line of sight, and embarrassment washes over me. Everyone who has ever come in here, including my own parents, have commented on the TV.

"A bit big, but considering the size of the room..." I try to justify.

Perhaps I did go a bit overboard in the past five years when business was booming. It's mostly paid off, but I probably should have taken it easy. I was just too keen to settle in a place of my own that would remind me of the house I grew up in. To prove that this unconventional career of mine could be as successful as Dad's law practice.

What the hell, why should I be ashamed? I earned every penny that's gone into this place. And yet, I now worry I'm sending the wrong message.

"Anyway, shall we order in something for dinner? Are you hungry?" I ask, trying to distract from the negativity that has crept back into my thoughts.

He shrugs. "Sure, what are the options?"

I get up to open the drawer of the coffee table, and retrieve a bunch of takeaway menus.

"The Chinese is particularly good, or there's always pizza."

While George picks through the leaflets, I wonder how long it will take for us to be more comfortable together. This weekend has seen a lot of firsts for both of us: the best picnic I've ever been to, me accepting someone else's offer of help rather than stubbornly struggling on my own. And finally, working together, which meant letting another person into my office. The latter was quite strange at first. I'm so used to living alone, that I'm not quite sure how people manage to relax with others around.

Despite being shattered after a hard day's work, still I'm restless. Like there's something I'm supposed to do tonight which has slipped my mind. I decide to check if I have other takeaway menus, perhaps in the kitchen drawer.

"Pizza sounds great," George greets me when I come back into the lounge empty-handed.

"Sure thing." I take the menu from him, as he mentions what he wants. Back in the hallway, I call to place the order.

As soon as I hang up, a realization hits me. *Shit.* It's Sunday evening, and my turn to phone Mum and Dad!

I stick my head around the doorway, cordless phone still in hand, and find George flipping through channels.

"Just a sec, I've got make another call."

He gives me the thumbs up.

Before I get the chance to say much else, the phone rings on its own. They've beat me to it.

"Hello?"

"Hey, Lucy, darling. We hadn't heard from you so thought we'd phone up instead." Dad sounds as cheerful as always on the other line.

"Sorry about that, I got tied up with an urgent project." And considering the company still spilling over from said project, I'm anxious to get off the line soon. I probably sound like it too.

"How's business?" Dad asks.

"You work too hard," Mum chimes in from the background. They must have me on speaker.

"Yeah, not bad, Dad. Things are picking up."

"Anyway, sweetheart, we were just wondering if you were planning anything for your thirty-fifth," Mum continues.

"Uhh right, my birthday..." Time sure has flown by. Last time we talked about it, I had said I'd organize something, a family get-together perhaps, and it's completely slipped my mind ever since. "Well, I suppose there's still time."

"Don't tell me you forgot!" Mum exclaims.

"Uhh... No, Mum, just..."

"She forgot, can you believe it, Bernard?"

Dad responds with a grunt, signaling he can believe it all too well. I sigh in defeat. This particular anecdote is no doubt going to be repeated in front of anyone who will listen for years to come. Barely five weeks to go, and this big project, I don't know how

I'll manage to organize a party as well.

"Anyway, I had an inkling this might happen, so I convinced your dad to make some enquiries at the club."

"Mum, you didn't have to!"

"Yes, darling, we did," Dad butts in.

"So, that's settled then. We'll let everyone know. You just turn up, all right, sweetie?" Mum says.

"Sure thing, Mum. Thanks so much."

"No problem. It will be nice to see everyone again. Otherwise we'll get to a stage where the only time we meet up as a family is at weddings and funerals."

"Indeed. Umm, mind if I call it a night-?" I'm about to say I've got company, but it seems wrong to announce that so early on, and will likely create questions. "I'm really beat after the week I've had."

"Of course, Lucy. We'll talk again next week. Take care of yourself, will you?"

"Bye, Mum, Dad," I say, before hanging up and finding George in front of me, empty glass in hand.

CHAPTER TWELVE

"Your folks?" he asks.

I nod and shoot him a sheepish smile.

"Shall I get us a refill while we wait for the food?" I ask.

He nods, and follows me to the kitchen, where he leans on a counter, while I get a couple more bottles out of the fridge.

"So... I couldn't help but overhear some of that. When is your birthday exactly? I can't believe I haven't asked yet."

"Oh, that. To be frank, I totally forgot about it. May first. Apparently Mum and Dad are throwing me a party and they're calling the whole family. I had told them I'd do it, but with everything that's been going on, it slipped my mind."

I pause for a moment, unsure whether to invite him or not. It's all a bit soon, isn't it? But then, he can always refuse.

"If you like, you're more than welcome to come... By then hopefully it'll be a double celebration. The project should be delivered." I focus on pouring his drink, avoiding eye contact. Great, now I'm nervous again, but I can't tell whether it's because I want him to say 'yes' or 'no'.

"It's going to be a big affair then?" he asks, nodding his thanks when I hand him the refilled pint glass.

"Sort of, they insisted that since it's kind of a milestone-"

George's raised eyebrows remind me that he hasn't got any clue what I'm on about.

"Sorry, it's my thirty-fifth. Ever since Dad's bypass, they feel any birthday should be celebrated, no exceptions. But those with a zero or a five in the end doubly so."

"Ah, right. Well, if you want me there, I'll come."

I look at him, trying to decipher his thoughts. He didn't sound all that keen, throwing the ball in my court, and yet, he looks his usual self, comfortable.

"I'll make sure you get an invite then," I say. "Cheers."

We walk back into the lounge where the TV is still on, showing a custom bike build mid-progress. It seems our tastes in television overlap nicely as well. Throw in an unhealthy compulsion to watch *Die Hard* every single time it's on, and we'll be golden.

"Umm... considering it's probably an hour's drive back for you, and the pizza is not going to come for at least another thirty minutes, would you like to stay?" I ask.

He sits down on the sofa right opposite the TV,

and pats on the seat beside him.

"One condition," he says.

"What's that?"

"You come here and relax." He takes my glass while I join him on the couch.

"You noticed that, huh?" I let out a deep sigh. "I'm just—well, I'm not used to having people over."

"I guessed as much." He hands me back my drink and puts his arm around me.

I look over at him, noting the amused glint in his eye.

"That's funny, is it? I thought it was kind of sad."

"It's funny, because I never get visitors either."

"And here I thought things were about to get awkward again. What with the oversized house, oversized TV and upcoming oversized birthday party." I put my glass down and lean back against him, closing my eyes.

"Well okay, all that is definitely a bit odd." He lets out a chuckle, which makes me smile too. "So tell me about your folks, what are they like?"

"Dad was a barrister, had his own firm right until his heart issues started some years back. Mum was at home with us. They still live a few villages over, in the same house where I grew up."

"So you have siblings?"

"Kind of. My cousin, Pete stayed with us from when he was ten. He's a few years older than me and always treated me like his little sister." Resting my hand on George's knee, I try hard to focus on the conversation, rather than our physical connection. "What about you? Tell me about your family."

He places his hand on top of mine, which makes me feel hot and cold at the same time, yet I dare not move.

"Grew up in Birmingham, my folks are still there. Dad worked at Longbridge, the car factory, all his life. Though he's a car guy, it's because of him that I got into motorcycles. The Harley, we built it together."

"That's really nice, to share something like that with your dad."

"I suppose. They weren't all that thrilled when I decided to get into IT though, and move down south."

"Mine weren't thrilled with my career choices either. Dad always wanted me to take over the firm from him. But law, it's just too dry for me."

George pulls me closer against him, and plants a kiss in my hair. How funny, the similarities between us, despite coming from vastly different backgrounds.

"Do you have any brothers or sisters?" I ask.

He shakes his head. "It's just me."

I turn to face him, and just look. It's funny, the more I get to know, the more familiar he becomes, the more time I could spend observing him.

"What?" he asks.

I have nothing more to say, so just smile.

"Stop staring at me." He tries to sound stern, but his eyes betray that he doesn't really mind.

"Make me."

No sooner do the words pass through my lips, than he jumps into action. He lifts me off the sofa, making me land astride him. Then he cups my face and guides it towards his. I try my best to stay alert, to not give in and instead drown in those blue eyes of his. But when our lips fuse, I have to admit defeat.

"Yep," I gasp.

"Mhm?"

"That'll do it."

It's infuriating, having to shut down so many of my emotions all day, then find a way to let them out after hours. A balancing act I'm not yet proficient at.

"What do you say we take this upstairs?" I suggest, just before diving into the crook of his neck.

"Too far," he says through gritted teeth while I start nibbling on his earlobe.

All day we've been together, his scent infiltrating my senses when I least expected it. In between the serious discussions about work, every so often his eyes would linger on me just enough to remind me that we're supposed to share more than work. But I had kept those emotions in check, as hard as it was.

And now, it's time to release everything, and yet I still hesitate. I need to stop playing boss or colleague or hostess and just be me.

"Why so tense?" George asks, his fingers exploring the rigid muscles on my shoulders.

I want to tell him everything that's been on my mind lately. From the mortgage payment reminders I've been trying to ignore, to my worries that us working together will hamper the more intimate nature of our relationship. Truthfully of course, I'd been tense way before I even met him, before Akhil left, ever since I haven't had a decent project in months. All of the rest is just adding to the mess.

"Work, you know. It never ends." I force a smile, then shut my eyes as his hands work their magic on me.

Maybe one day I'll tell him everything that's been on my mind. But not today. I don't want to face it.

Opening my eyes again, I lean down for a kiss, only to find him as intensely hungry for me as I am for him. He peels off my t-shirt, letting my hair cascade down over the naked skin on my shoulders and cleavage. I look back up at him, and hook my finger under his shirt as well.

Your turn.

He hesitates just a bit, so little that a casual observer might not have noticed, but I do. My fingers start work on his buttons, revealing more tempting skin as I progress upwards. Seeing the dragon tattoo on his shoulder again makes me want one of my own.

ONE NIGHT STAND

I wonder if he likes girls with tattoos as well.

I dive down, kissing, licking, nibbling my way down his torso. Soft, warm skin, burning into my lips. Lust surges within me, making it hard to be gentle, when what I really want to do is claw, bite, suck and tear. It's hard to explain, to analyze why when you're engrossed in someone, you feel a need to own them, sometimes even to hurt them, because it's the only way to release the tension inside.

Of course I don't hurt him, not much anyway, looking at the feverish expression on his face. He's ready, he wants this as much as me.

His fingers dig into my ass, his teeth gently surround the nipple he has just freed from my bra. Items of clothing, discarded on the ground one by one, until we're both naked.

He's brought condoms, of course he has, and puts one on in a rush so we can progress. Soon we may not need them, it's the ultimate sign of trust to forgo all barriers.

When I lower myself onto him, I imagine what he'll feel like unsheathed, how much better it will be. If that's even possible. Had he not made the first move, I may have let things progress without the rubber already. I want him. Closer, skin against skin, deeper as well as harder.

The leather of the sofa sticks against our skin, causing a hot prickling sensation whenever we move.

Funny how the things that are annoying while watching TV can be such a turn on during sex. Pain and pleasure are related like incestuous cousins.

He lifts me with every thrust, causing me to bounce up and down on him higher and faster than I could manage on my own. The tension that has been building all day, in between the chats, emails, spreadsheets and briefings is trying its best to claw its way out of my chest. His too, his eyes seem to burn with a lust more intense than words could express.

"Cum for me, Lucy," he groans. "I love to see the pleasure written all over your face."

I'm done holding back, done being proper or professional. For him, I want to be it all, a saint in the day, slut at night. I fuck him with renewed energy, to make it so he's unable to talk, just like me. Our means of communication is limited to thrusts, groans, moans and screams.

He bucks his hips, his brow furrowed and lips slightly parted. More kisses, more caresses. I grab hold of his neck, anchoring myself down with every movement. Until I lose it, and die a thousand deaths in his arms, only to be reborn, sweaty and exhausted, as well as sated.

Just at the moment when my thighs threaten to give way, he tenses up, making me continue on, fighting to keep moving, to push him over the edge with me. His cock seems to grow and pulsate inside me. His pleasure infects me again, making me shiver from the inside out, and I cry out again, taking his full length inside me until everything subsides for the second time.

Not just my thighs, but all of me gives up and all the sound left in this room is a roar of an engine behind us. The bike builders on TV finally managed to get their creation started it seems.

"Did you just..." George asks, while panting for air. His arms wrap around me again, gentler this time.

"Twice," I whisper, unable or unwilling to move.

"Wow."

CHAPTER THIRTEEN

The sound of my phone alarm wakes me, but I struggle to emerge from the fog straightaway. Across me, tucking me safely into my duvet, George's arm serves as protection against the inconvenient outside world. He stayed over, and unlike the first time we fell asleep in the same bed, last night wasn't interrupted by sleepless doubts on my part.

"Morning," he whispers in my ear, making the prospect of getting up even less tempting than it already was.

I blink against the light filtering through the gaps in the curtains, and wait for reality to come into focus.

"Morning."

The peace and quiet is now ruined by my alarm clock, which is set to come on mere minutes after the phone, just in case the former doesn't rouse me. Another day lies ahead, but one which is set to start just a bit differently.

"Back to the grind, eh?" George stretches, letting go of me in the process.

Suddenly overly aware of my nakedness underneath the sheets, I wrap them tighter around myself.

"Unfortunately. Staying in bed would have been much more fun."

I turn around, resting my hand on the dragon tattoo on his shoulder which I've spent a lot of last night familiarizing myself with. What is it with men and tattoos, that makes them infinitely sexier than men without tattoos? And long-haired, big men with tattoos... My mind instantly shows me a replay of some of last night's more poignant moments. Sweaty, sticky, delicious moments that they were.

The phone goes off again, as it will do every minute until I shut down the alarm completely.

"Sorry about that." I struggle with the touch screen in my half-dazed state, wondering if perhaps it would be best to throw it against a wall if it doesn't stop screaming straightaway.

"Needs must." George starts to get up, and I stay back and watch as he picks up his t-shirt and boxers off the floor.

"Bathroom's this one, right?" He points at the door on the left, next to the one leading to the walk-in closet.

"That's right."

"This house is too damn big and confusing," he mumbles, as he steps inside.

"I can draw you a map if you want," I joke behind him just before he shuts the door.

Whew, that was... amazing, different, out of

character, and a bit scary. It's also coming up on the most time I've ever spent with another human being not directly related to me.

***

"So..." I look up from my screen, and struggle not to let my voice crack while making light of the shit storm that's about to unfold. "I've got good news and bad news."

"Start with the good."

"The prep work for the presentation is going to finish a lot sooner than expected."

"What's the bad part?" George asks.

"He wants to meet today, at one. Apparently he's been called away for the rest of the week and wants to settle things before then."

He looks at me, I look at him. "I'm beginning to understand why you keep referring to him as the Nightmare Client."

"Right. Is it even possible? We're so not ready yet."

"Four hours," George mumbles, while checking the clock on the wall behind me. "Where?"

"Pretty close to where we first met, Waterloo."

"Fuck." He runs his hand over his hair. "Sorry."

"I know."

"And how far exactly would that be from here?"

"Little over an hour by train, plus about forty-five

minutes total to get to Reading Station from here, and walk to his restaurant from Waterloo."

"I am so glad I already had a shower."

"Tell me about it." My shoulders slump down, and I rest my face on my fists. Perhaps it's time to admit defeat.

"Please tell me you have two laptops hidden away in this place somewhere?" George pushes his chair back and walks the few steps towards me, leaning over and resting his hand on my back. "If we can keep working on the train, we may be able to wing it."

I raise my head, to find him looking down at me. His lips pressed together in determination, and a thoughtful frown to match.

"Do you really think so?" I ask.

"You don't suppose he would give us a little leeway, considering he moved up the meeting?"

I shrug. "Maybe, though as far as he knows we've been working as a team for ages."

"True. Well then, we'll just have to act confident enough together to convince him."

George smiles down at me, causing all kinds of warm, fuzzy feelings. If he really thinks we can do it, perhaps it's worth a shot. There's a lot at stake for me, but if we don't try at least, all is already lost.

"There's a sample follow-up presentation Akhil made in the Documents folder, perhaps it helps. I'll see about those laptops."

I get up and head straight towards the large filing cabinet by the window. I don't like working on a laptop, especially when doing graphics, but sometimes you do need something more portable than a workstation with a twenty-three-inch screen. It doesn't take long for me to find the new one, but my back-up is proving more difficult to locate.

"I've got an older one too, but I think it may be in the attic. Give me a moment?" I ask.

George nods without looking up from his work. "Take your time, I'm going to make a start on this."

It takes me a solid fifteen minutes of rummaging through old boxes full of documents and other business stuff in the attic to locate the other laptop. Fifteen minutes that I wasn't able to spend preparing and left George to his own devices downstairs.

Another fifteen minutes get wasted trying to upgrade Office so at least we can share the same documents between us.

This second meeting will be the one to convince a control-freak micro-manager that we can indeed deliver to his highly accelerated time frame. People often say once they call you back, that's most of the battle won. For our sake, and for the sake of my bank balance, I hope that's the case.

We keep our heads down, working away with no breaks until it's time to leave. George is forced to wear whatever he was wearing yesterday, which thankfully did feature a button-up shirt of sorts, even if it is denim. How lucky he keeps a beard, so the issue of shaving doesn't come up. I opt for a trouser suit, so at least one of us looks the part.

Before we know it, most of our prep time is over, and we find ourselves on a train zipping through fields and villages, on our way into the capital. It's the same journey I made for the first meeting, before George and I had even met.

Although there is a significant chance we're not ready, we're unwilling to give up either. Our backs are against the wall—at least mine is—and we have no choice anymore but to move forward. The adrenaline has kicked in, and not even the shrieking teenage girls in the row of seats behind us can break our focus.

As our train pulls into Waterloo, we rush to pack up our things and start walking, with me leading the way while still rehearsing parts of the presentation. We arrive at Cleary's with ten minutes to spare, and the front door opens the second we arrive.

"Lovely to see you," Jack Cleary greets me with a handshake, while scrutinizing George, who's towering over the both of us more like a bodyguard than anything else.

"This is George, my project manager." I'm still trying to catch my breath after the brisk walk from the station, as is he.

"I see. Please do come in." Cleary turns on his heel

after shaking George's hand briefly.

George gives me a quick look, and a shrug. While I've thrown on a business suit as usual, of course George doesn't quite project the same image. I like to think that's okay, considering he's a techie. It's all about attitude from here on.

As soon as we move into Cleary's office, some glasses of water appear and we're on the clock. He hasn't got much time, and neither do I wish to drag out this already stressful and uncomfortable situation. We get right down to business, explaining the revised timeline, and suggested milestones along the way. George takes over, running through the PowerPoint like a total pro, allowing me to fall back and just observe.

I'm impressed.

By the end, so is Cleary.

I hand over the paperwork, which he signs without hesitation, then he hands me a check and we're escorted out of the office, and restaurant, before getting the chance to say or think anything else.

"Whoa..." George lets out a sigh, as we find ourselves, rather helplessly, on the pavement outside just when the clouds threaten to burst open with the first droplets of rain. In all this rush, neither of us thought to carry a decent coat or umbrella.

"That went well." I straighten myself, stretching achy back muscles; a reminder of just how stressed I have been for weeks. "Thank you so much."

I rest my hand on his arm, and am rewarded with heavier raindrops landing square in my face.

"Screw this. Let's have lunch somewhere, celebrate. I think we deserve a bit of a break after all that. From tomorrow, the real work starts."

He nods, but doesn't say anything more. The rain speeds up, forcing a quick decision.

"How about this place?" I point at an inviting glass frontage, with rustic looking wooden tables and chairs inside. It's not very busy, but there are enough people inside to suggest the food may be edible.

"Sure. Hey, you go ahead, I'll be just behind you," George says, his hand stuck firmly in his pocket.

I shrug and head inside, getting a table for the two of us halfway towards the back of the little bistro. After casting off my jacket, and attempting to shake off most of the water from it, I sit, facing the windows. It's significantly darker outside than only a moment ago. In good old British fashion, the weather has made a U-turn for the worse in mere minutes.

"Can I take your order?" a very cheerful female voice with a hint of a Mediterranean accent asks beside me.

"I'm waiting for someone. Just a coffee for now, thanks."

In an attempt to pass the time, I decide to respond to Callum Byrne, asking him when he would like to meet to discuss the project. Meanwhile, my coffee arrives, allowing me to warm up a little.

What's taking George so long?

It's only by the time I'm done with the email, as well as most of my coffee, when he enters, stuffing his phone back into his pocket. Good. I'm starving, as I imagine he is too.

CHAPTER FOURTEEN

Another day, another boatload of work. We may have convinced Cleary to hand over his advance, but that's only the beginning. Now the real job starts.

George arrived early, after staying the night at his place. The roar of his Harley no doubt woke the entire neighborhood, it certainly made me take notice. I was slightly disappointed he didn't want to stay with me after lunch yesterday, but I can't really expect him to stop going home altogether.

I still have to broach the topic of his job somehow. How is he managing the time off? I can't imagine your average employer would be pleased to find out that their staff has started taking days without notice just so they can work with someone else in the same industry. Then again, he assured me it's fine, perhaps I ought to trust him.

There's not much time for idle chat now. We have to put the timeline he had prepared with Neeraj earlier into action. Everyone has a job to do, so now they have to be informed, and managed, so everything remains on schedule.

It's been a very long time since I worked in an actual office environment, but I imagine it's something similar to the set-up we have now, just with more people. At the spare desk, George is briefing Neeraj and a couple of the other guys by Skype, while I'm catching up on a bit of admin work. Within days, he's been able to fill the gap Akhil left, and more.

I'm actually starting to relax a little, which is unusual at the beginning of a new job. Normally, I don't allow myself to become too comfortable until the end is in sight.

The phone rings, a London number, which I decide to take in the other room to get away from George's chatter in the background. It's Callum Byrne. Ordinarily I'd be tense, having two such important jobs overlap slightly but George's involvement has made me confident the current project will be on track. As a result, I'm pleased Byrne called back so soon after my email.

Now, we agree that I work on a proposal for him, to be presented in person when he's back from some sourcing trip to Italy a few weeks from now. Things sound extremely promising, and I can't wait to share the good news.

When I return to the office, George isn't at his seat, his briefing must have finished. I decide to wait, answering a few emails, after which I begin to sketch a few rough ideas for the Cleary website. After around five minutes, impatience starts to grow in me.

ONE NIGHT STAND

Deep breaths, you can't expect him to be glued to his chair twelve hours a day! He's not me, after all.

I know I'm being unreasonable, and yet...

When he comes back, mobile phone in hand, he seems a lot less cheerful than I just was after the chat with Byrne.

"You alright?" I ask.

"Yeah, fine. Hey, if you don't have anything else for me to do right now, do you mind if I duck out for a bit?"

Wonder what that's about.

"The guys are on task?"

"Yeah, just a matter of them doing the work now, I should probably check in with them for daily updates though."

"Good idea. Well, why not take the day? I feel kind of bad for taking up all your time lately."

"Thanks, Lucy. See you tomorrow," George says, the relief evident in his eyes.

Wonder what all that was about. I watch him as he packs up his things, and get up myself to see him out. He's rather quiet, all the way down the stairs. I don't ask what's the matter, because I don't want to pry. This whole dynamic, him asking for time and me suggesting he '*take the day*', is all very cold to me. We're working together now, so technically he's an employee at least for the time being.

But he's not, really, is he?

"Later," I say, unsure of whether to kiss him goodbye, or what else to do.

He nods, then puts on his helmet before starting his bike and speeding out of the gate.

When I get back upstairs and sit down to continue working, the silence of my now empty office is deafening.

***

"Hey, just wondering whether you'd like to have dinner tonight," I speak into the phone.

The crackle on the other end of the line is distracting, while I wait for his response.

Now that work on the back-end development of the website project is in full swing, I've needed less and less of George's time. So much so, that I insisted he stop sitting around my place every day, and go back to his regular job. Despite his protests, I couldn't imagine how anyone would be able to get that much time off without consequences.

And so, for the past two weeks, he's been handling the daily briefings and updates mostly from home.

Things are rolling along nicely, and I've assured him it won't change his share of the profits. But it has meant we've seen less and less of each other, while I've been neck deep in my part of the project, as well as prep work for the next one. Those times we did meet up, he seemed distant. No matter what we started talking about, our conversations always ended up being about work in the end.

Things just haven't been the same. And I couldn't help noticing that he always seemed to keep one eye on his phone when we were together.

"Dinner? Out or in?" George asks.

I hadn't considered that yet, but the answer presents itself in the paperwork on my desk.

"Well, how about we go somewhere nice? The new client, Byrnc, has a restaurant in Henley. We could check it out, and I'll write it off as research, what do you say?"

The line is quiet for a bit, except for the continuous interference.

"Come on, it's a nice ride to get there too. We could take both the bikes this time."

"Alright then. I'll be at your place at seven."

With a click, even the persistent crackle in the line goes silent.

Is it just my imagination or did he seem less than thrilled by the prospect of going out tonight? Or perhaps I'm just projecting my own doubts and worries onto him?

After the intense early days we spent together, picking up the pieces Akhil left behind, all the business stuff is getting in the way of *us*. It has been hard to pick things up where we left them, romantically. Even our emails back and forth have changed drastically in tone. It's all business, no play, and it's been getting me down.

I need to turn things around and tonight could be the time to do it. And perhaps we'll do better once we can focus on us as a couple, rather than this impromptu working relationship we've found ourselves in. Things are going well, we've been on target for all the milestones set in the initial schedule for the Cleary project, including getting him to sign off my design.

There's only one thing I can think to do to fix this: I'm going to draw a line under it all. I'll cut a check and see if George and I can find our way back to how it all started. Just two regular people, who found each other by chance. Time to take the business nonsense out of the equation. I'm sure I can take over now that most of the work is done.

Despite planning to go for a ride this evening, I decide to dress up a bit. Skinny jeans and a nice top with a plunging neckline, to remind him of what we shared before work got in the way. Just enough make-up to show I've made an effort, and even some jewelry. I don't recall the last time I even wore earrings since all of this began.

It's been weeks since we've truly been ourselves, or so it seems. Like we've both forgotten how much we share, other than one silly project that's going to be over before we know it.

I wonder if he's even still interested in me? Could it be that we just didn't click as well as I thought? Perhaps our connection was one-sided from the start, and I just didn't realize it?

I try to shake these unhelpful thoughts, and while away the time until seven o'clock. But no matter what I do to distract myself, the doubts keep on returning.

By the time he turns up, I've been ready for half an hour, pacing about the place just like the first time we were going to go on a ride together. Although we know each other better now, it still feels like I've barely scratched the surface and I just can't tell where his head is at mostly.

"Hey, I'll be right out," I tell George over the intercom when he reaches the gate.

He gives me the thumbs-up and returns to his bike.

I gather up my helmet and gloves, and head out to warm up my bike. The Honda's engine doesn't roar like George's Harley, rather it shrieks, especially at higher revs. *Like a banshee,* the thought makes me smile. It goes like one too, I have no doubts that I'll not only be able to keep up with George, but outrun him. They're different beasts, much like him and me, even if they're both bikes of a similar age.

After a couple of minutes, I can't wait any longer and get in the saddle, joining George outside the gate.

With a nod, I speed off the drive and onto the road, with him hot on my heels.

This time of day is just right for a little ride. Most of the office rush fizzles out by about six-thirty, leaving the way through Reading quiet enough to make it enjoyable. Then, once the countryside opens up, it's like entering a different world.

I let him know where to go with the odd hand signal, but the road signs are self-explanatory. We take turns leading, overtaking one another with either a growl or a scream from our exhausts. By the time we reach, I can't wipe my smile off my face. Although he had seemed unenthusiastic at first on the phone, when we park up at Byrne's restaurant, his eyes have lit up as well.

We weren't meant to sit in an office together. This—riding through winding rural roads together— is what we were meant to do!

"Hungry?" I ask.

"Famished," he responds, while trying to get his wild, long mane under control after taking off his helmet.

CHAPTER FIFTEEN

I can't take my eyes off him as we sit down. Earlier worries, forgotten while on the road together, come creeping back into my thoughts. The check is in my pocket, I just have to find the right time to bring it up, and to make it so there is no misunderstanding my intentions.

This is the right call, isn't it? I just want things to work out somehow, he must realize that.

He's studying the offerings, while I pretend to look at the specials board behind him. Actually, I keep glancing down, taking in every detail of his features. Even though we're sitting down, he still looks tall. And broad. And irresistible.

His blue eyes, so focused on the menu, I can't look at them without remembering the first moment we truly seemed to connect. That was not long ago at all, only a few weeks, and yet everything is so different now.

I remember that night so clearly, how we'd started flirting almost reluctantly, how surprisingly shy he turned out to be once we were alone. And then, all of a sudden, all hesitation vanished, when our beings came together spectacularly. It was as if subconsciously we both decided to ignore all sense and reason, and just give in to pleasure.

For years I've been alone and not really felt like I was missing out. Now I know I have been. I want more of this in my life. Someone to spend time with. To make it seem worthwhile to sit down in a nice place together, whiling the hours away with good food and better conversation.

I want to feel wanted, and needed. And... loved. Surely, that's what everyone wants? He would too?

"Have you decided?" George looks up, snapping me out of my wishful thinking.

"Umm, steak. I could murder a good steak." It's the first thing that popped into my head, probably because part of my research on Callum Byrne involved watching a few snippets of his TV show, one of which about steak.

"Sounds good. I'll have the same thing." George shuts the leather binder containing the menu, and leans back, checking out our surroundings. "I don't think I've ever been at a TV chef's restaurant before."

I smile, and follow his gaze towards a photograph of the man in question, hanging above the bar counter. With his carefully styled hair and blindingly white teeth, Callum Byrne's picture looks like a TV still, not at all like a real person.

"I'm sure whatever they're serving, it's just food."

He shrugs. "At least they wrote down the weight

of the steak, so they can't get away with plating up half a bite of meat, while charging all that money for *presentation*."

I let out a chuckle, and allow myself to relax. Might as well broach the subject.

"Say, George," I start, waiting for his attention to move away from the various certificates and awards lined up on the wall beside us, and back to me.

"Yeah?"

"I've been thinking about us, working together." No matter how hard I try to convince myself it's all for the best, still my heart starts to pound. What if he takes it the wrong way?

"It's been rather stressful, and intense, hasn't it?" I ask.

"Not too bad."

"Well I just feel like we've just been talking about work and nothing else."

George leans back in his seat, his eyes only on me now. I have his full attention, and still, I can't read him at all.

"How about we start over? Just you and me. No work, no clients, no distractions?" My voice cracks slightly, betraying my nerves. It's the moment of truth, this can either go the way I want it to, or completely to hell.

"I'm not sure I understand."

I find the check in my pocket, extracting it

carefully and place it on the table right in between us.

"The amount is what we agreed. You know how people say not to bring money into relationships? Well, I wanted to get it out of the way."

He picks it up, and frowns.

"I thought things were going well with the project?"

"Yeah, they are. Everything is going perfectly. But I don't like thinking of you as an employee, you know? And as long as this job is hanging over our heads..." I explain, but the look on his face tells me he's not on the same page. Rather than an attempt to save our relationship, he's seeing it as a judgment of his work.

"George, you have been absolutely invaluable." I reach over to touch his hand, which twitches slightly when my fingers connect with his. "I want something more intimate with you than a working relationship. Lately, I've been wondering if perhaps I can't have both."

"I see." He removes his hand from underneath mine, to fold the check in half and put it in his shirt pocket. "Well, I guess you've made your choice."

I try to look him in the eye, to figure out just how he feels, but he's avoiding my gaze. My heart sinks, but I don't let it scare me off. I need to make him understand somehow.

"All I'm saying is, I want you in my life. Not just in

my office." My eyes are getting moist, causing me to blink a few times. "I really like you, George."

He nods, then just sits there, quietly. I want to press him for a reaction, to find out whether he feels the same, but part of me is too afraid to ask. Instead, I just hold my breath, forcing my emotions back in check.

"Your order, please?" An impeccably dressed waiter has appeared out of nowhere, clutching one of those electronic machines that sends the order straight to the kitchen.

I wait for George to take the lead, just in case he wants to forget about dinner and leave. The few seconds of silence make my heart skip a whole lot of beats, but then, he collects himself.

"Two steak platters, please. A coke for me, and you?" He gestures at me.

"Same. A coke."

The waiter disappears almost as quickly as he had shown up earlier.

"I was worried you'd want to leave," I whisper.

"Nah, I'm not going anywhere until I try this guy's steak." George shoots me a wry smile.

I've hurt him, but the fact that he's still here means he's trying to see things my way. Perhaps we can move on from here after all. Onwards and upwards.

Throughout dinner, and the mind-blowing dessert that follows, we don't talk much. I ask him a few necessary questions about work, the last ones I hope, just so I can take over from tomorrow. Beyond that, suddenly it seems like we have nothing to say.

It's only temporary, I try to convince myself, *we're transitioning and then everything will be fine.*

But when we get ready to leave, and I ask if he wants to have a coffee at mine, things are not yet fine. He refuses. I ask when I'll see him again, and he doesn't commit either way.

Perhaps I need to give him some time to digest this new situation. Yes, that's it. I'll give him some space, and time. If we are meant to be, things will work themselves out.

***

"So it's all set then," I say, waiting for Callum Byrne's reaction on the other end of the phone.

"Indeed. Monday, nine am. Will your project manager be joining us?"

His question makes me pause. Dammit, why does he have to bring up George now?

"It'll just be me."

"Oh, that's too bad. Jack was very impressed by him."

Cleary told him, of course! The two of them do seem to be very close, it's only obvious that they'd discuss the project, and our meetings, in detail, even if

I now wish they hadn't.

"George is actually focusing on Jack Cleary's project at the moment, making sure everything is completed on time. Hence he won't be attending the meeting." It's the best justification I could come up with, though in truth I have no idea what George is up to. Our contact since dinner last week has been strained at best. If I had time to let my imagination get the better of me, I would say he was avoiding me.

"Oh well, maybe next time, eh?" Byrne says.

"Indeed. Looking forward to meeting you on Monday."

"Likewise." With that, Byrne hangs up, leaving me lost in thoughts.

I should reach out to George, see how he's doing. Surely a week should be enough time to think things through and realize I decided what I did to help us, not make things worse between us? Then again, I have been incredibly busy myself, so I shouldn't just blame him for not keeping in touch.

It's early Friday evening, perhaps he's just leaving the office now. Let's see if he's free to talk, or willing to meet up tonight.

I dial his number, and wait. Switched off. Maybe he's still at work then, oh well.

Instead of obsessing about George, I decide to finish off some emails. The Byrne proposal is as good as done, and the Cleary project is racing towards the finish line. Thanks to George's help with the freelancers, things have been going relatively smoothly.

I shoot off an email to Neeraj, asking him to confirm the proposed timeline for the Byrne project, the last piece of the puzzle, before the proposal can be sent off in preparation for Monday's meeting. It's quite late in India, so I don't expect a response until the morning. However, just when I'm about to try George's number again, a response does come in. It's just a single sentence from Neeraj:

Where is George?

Goddammit!

When I took over last week, I did explain that George had work of his own to go back to, so I'd handle things myself again. His reaction had been skeptical at first, but then he dropped the issue. Now, it seems his curiosity is getting the better of him again.

There's only one problem: it's none of his business. It's none of anyone's business. From the start, I'd made it clear that George was helping out temporarily, so why can't people just drop it? If Byrne's question wasn't already irritating enough, now this. This is my company, has been from the start, and yet it seems like I'm the fucking third wheel. How is that fair, after all the years I've killed myself to grow this business?

Jesus Christ.

I'm dangerously close to losing my cool, but decide to pound out a quick response to Neeraj anyway.

Never mind George, what about the schedule I asked about?

He'd been quick enough to reply last time, so I sit there, my heart still pounding in my throat, and cheeks burning up. No matter how hard I stare at the screen, nothing else comes in. No confirmation, not even a repeat of the same question.

I'm about to lose it and send another, harsher email, when my phone interrupts me.

"Hello," I all but bark into the phone.

"Hey, George here. You called?"

Deep breaths, don't say anything you'll regret later.

"Oh, yeah, sorry. I just wanted to ask what's going on. If perhaps you're free to talk, or meet up or something?" I want to sound genuine, agreeable, but it's hard to get over my earlier frustration.

There's a pause, filled with the familiar crackle I always seem to get when calling George's mobile number. Keeping the phone wedged between my ear and shoulder, I rub my temples and focus on calm, slow breaths.

"Lucy..." George starts, his voice breaking up slightly with interference.

"Yeah?"

"I don't think this is going to work."

His words hit me like a blow to the gut. Is everything destined to go to shit within one day?

"What do you mean?" I ask.

"My folks, you know they've never been happy about me living so far away, plus they're not getting any younger. It's time I moved closer to them. Just thought I should let you know."

"You're leaving? When?"

"Next week."

I'm speechless, and still riled up after the emails earlier, but now I'm starting to see red. *What the fuck?*

"And you thought you should let me know, now, after *I* called *you*. That's fucking great."

"I'm sorry, Lucy. I never meant to hurt you."

"This is not happening. You don't get to do this over the phone. Are you home?"

"Yes."

"I'm coming over." I hang up and throw the phone onto my desk in disgust.

CHAPTER SIXTEEN

Throughout the drive to George's place, I'm reeling with conflicting emotions. Sure, things were complicated lately, but I still hoped we could get past it. But instead of making an effort, he drops a bomb of epic proportions on me. Finally, here's a guy I could imagine having a relationship with, who seemed reliable at least at first, but in the end, you can't depend on anyone but yourself. I should've known.

Despite the rush hour traffic, which for some reason is so much worse on Fridays, my bike makes it into town in record time. Anger does that to a person: it makes you speed up when the most rational thing would be to slow down. I'm not entirely sure where I'm going, so I'm relying entirely on the SatNav to take me there.

Broad A-roads make way for smaller streets, turning off into a quieter residential area. The identical looking boxy houses are crammed together, window after window covered with net curtains, blocking their inhabitants from my view. I guess George's place must look something like this, since apparently I'm about to reach.

In a hundred yards, turn right.

On the corner, a group of teenagers stand around their scooters and smoke, while observing me. They can't tell from here of course, but I truly feel the outsider in what can only be described as a rougher part of town. Like if they'll figure it out, they'll pounce on me to punish my intrusion.

Your destination is on your left.

I look up from the SatNav, and check behind me to make sure the youths aren't following, before turning the key to switch off the engine. The house number, 23B, greets me on the concrete grey wall. There's a wonky *To Let* sign planted in the grassy bit next to the pavement. Inside, all looks dark and there is no movement. He'd better be here like he said!

Scanning the surroundings, I spy what looks like a two-wheeler, his I assume, protected by a grey waterproof cover, and a paper stuck on the front: *For Sale, call for more details*. Weird.

Just when I take off my helmet, letting my hair fall down over my shoulders, and stuff my gloves into my pocket, the dark curtain on the first floor twitches slightly. Shortly after, the click of a lock and creak of a door follows, putting me back on task. I will have my answers, soon, I will know what the hell is going on!

"So you found it all right," George remarks from the top of the exposed staircase, leading to the first floor. His tense expression makes all the muscles in my body turn rigid, preparing for a fight.

ONE NIGHT STAND

"Can I come in?" I say, while trying to keep my breathing under control. My cheeks are turning flushed, my blood truly is boiling.

He steps aside as I climb the stairs, and leads me inside, closing the door behind us. Despite the half-dark in his cramped hallway, I can make out the silhouettes of cardboard boxes. He's almost completely packed, I can't fucking believe it! The only items left out are a small side table with a phone and a big stack of torn open envelopes, plus their contents.

"Now tell me what you have to tell me." I put my hands on my hips and glare upwards. He's towering over me but I couldn't be less intimidated.

"Look." He sighs and avoids my angry stare. "It's been nice and all, but you and I both know this wasn't going to work out anyway."

"Bullshit. From where I'm standing, we had something special, at least before we started working together. I was trying to get that back, was giving you space to see things my way, except you suddenly decide to leave. If your parents do need you to move back up north, that's fine, we could have worked something out. But to just give up now..." I'm starting to sweat, despite the chill in his apartment. It's a good thing he doesn't have his heating on, or I'd really boil over. "And to not even let me know in advance, Jesus Christ, I expected more from you!"

"Well, maybe you shouldn't have."

"Clearly!" I take a deep breath, before allowing myself to voice what I really want to know. "Who is she?"

"What?"

"Don't even. You think I didn't notice? When we just landed the Cleary project, you were glued to your phone, checking messages or whatever, typing things when you thought I wasn't looking, hiding yourself away to take mysterious calls. And now you just want to end things without giving us a chance, it's the only logical explanation!"

Throughout the drive here, I kept analyzing every moment we had spent together, and I couldn't pinpoint exactly where things went bad. Sure, working together had made things weird, and last week's dinner was uncomfortable, but those can't be the only reasons, can they? We'd also spent a lot of happy moments together.

"That..." He runs his hand through his hair, and just stands there with his mouth half-open, but no explanation is forthcoming.

"Just tell me this. Was it already going on when we first met?"

"No... I..."

"Because if so, I really have to get my head examined. I can't believe how easily I fell for your lies." Tears prickle in my eyes, making my vision hazy.

I rest my hand against the wall, flexing my fingers,

which ache after being balled into a tight fist for the past five minutes. I try my best not to punch something or someone. Him.

I don't even know when I've last been so angry, so hurt. Betrayed. The whole Akhil incident has nothing on this.

"There is no one."

"Bullshit."

"Look, I understand you're angry, and not likely to believe a word I say. Look at me." George reaches over and guides my chin upwards, but I close my eyes to hide the accumulating tears.

I shake him off, and try to blink the wetness away, which sadly has the opposite effect. "Then why?"

He steps through the doorway, into the darkened living area, gesturing at me to follow. Inside, yet more cardboard boxes await us, and random clothes, strewn over the only item of furniture left: a shabby sofa.

I enter behind him, and sit down, without bothering to move any of the mess aside. What do I care? I came here for an explanation, not to be his fucking housekeeper.

George, meanwhile, leans against a tall stack of boxes across from the sofa, where one would have expected a TV to be. I check the room once more, noting the outlines of what might have been picture frames, faded into the wall. This place really could do with a lick of paint. No wonder he's never invited me over.

"Why, George? It couldn't have been what I said at dinner last week, could it? Nobody decides to move in less than a week! I know the Cleary project started out a total cluster fuck, but then, you offered to help yourself." My earlier rage is starting to dissipate, with desperation appearing in its place. Am I really that clueless that I can't tell whether a guy is even interested in me? Am I that hopeless? Perhaps I am better off alone.

"I haven't been entirely honest with you. From the start." His words pierce me like a knife. Here it comes, the confession.

I press my lips together, fearing what he'll say next. Whatever it is, I'll endure it. I can't let this break me.

"That night, when we first met, it was sort of my farewell from the job."

Wait, what?

"Go on," I say, confused whether this is yet more bullshit or the beginning of an actual explanation.

"I was let go, made redundant. It was my last day, so afterwards I went to the pub, feeling sorry for myself. I had planned to just drink, to forget the fact that my asshole of a manager had kept Steve, who is an incompetent twat, while choosing to fire me."

I'm speechless. This is the big reveal? He could've just said something, I would've understood. People are losing their jobs all over the place nowadays.

"And then, you came along, and I felt like maybe things would work out somehow, that the only reason I even lost the job was so I'd go to that particular pub on that particular night, you know?"

I'm not sure that I do know, but I choose to keep quiet.

"So instead of moping around, I decided I'd pull myself together, apply for whatever job I could, to find something as soon as possible—hence the phone calls."

Now that my eyes are more used to the darkness, I can see George staring at me from across the room. Even though I don't want to let him affect me, it's still giving me goose bumps to know he's looking right at me.

"But then, as I found out more about you, I just didn't see a way it would ever work out. Sure, we get on, we share some interests, but I could never measure up. Towards the end, I was sort of hoping you'd keep me on, but that's no basis for a relationship."

"None of this makes any sense," I mumble to myself.

He's breaking up with me because he doesn't have work? How stupid does he think I am?

He shrugs, and crosses his arms.

"You expect me to believe that you would choose to leave, just because you haven't found a job yet?"

"It's not *just* that."

"And what do you mean 'measure up'? I don't understand."

"We live in different worlds, you and I. You're a nice middle class girl, living in a nice middle class neighborhood in the countryside, surrounded by lawyers and bankers. Meanwhile, I've had to give notice on this shit hole because I won't be able to pay the rent anymore. You deserve so much more."

Holy shit. That explains the 'for sale' sign on his bike. How did I not put two and two together? But then, there's still one problem.

"So why didn't you cash the fucking check?" I exclaim. "And why not just be honest? What the hell, George! We were supposed to be honest with each other." That last bit almost makes me bite my tongue. How can I accuse him of dishonesty when I haven't been totally straight with him either?

"Because I didn't help you for the money. It felt... wrong."

Anger, made way for sadness, now I'm well on my way towards denial. I'm about to lose my mind, and yet a part of me still wants to believe.

What if...

"Okay. Tell me one thing. And if you say 'no', I'll drop the whole thing and let you get on with-" I gesture around the haphazardly stacked boxes. "Whatever. The move."

"Fair enough. What's that?" Right now, with his shoulders hanging down, he looks about as small as I've ever seen him, even if he's still impossibly tall. I'm reminded of the first time we met, how I somehow felt he was trustworthy, kind, and I wonder if perhaps I wasn't wrong about him after all.

"Deep down, and please be honest this time: if I lived down the road from you, same person, same interests, same everything, except the business. Different circumstances. Would that change anything? Would you still be breaking up with me?"

He looks down at his shoes and hesitates. Meanwhile I hold my breath and my heartbeat is going into overdrive. If his answer is negative, I'm certain I'll lose my composure entirely and cry my eyes out, right here in his living room.

"I guess not. But that's just hypothetical."

I let out a partial sigh of relief, hoping my next question gets a similar reaction.

"And what if, I was still the nice middle class girl that I am, living in the nice middle class neighborhood with the bankers and lawyers, who—before you rescued her restaurant project—was looking at having her nice middle class house repossessed by the bank?" I hadn't allowed myself to voice this terrifying possibility, ever since the reminders started coming a couple of months ago, it had been too painful. But now I must admit, it's a relief to have it out in the open.

"What?" George whispers, unable to hide the shock at my admission.

"Cleary's project. I didn't want to take it because he seemed so difficult from the start, but I had no choice. Business has been really slow for *months*. I've been behind on my mortgage since December."

"You're joking." George slowly rubs his chin, yet does not take his eyes off me.

"Everything isn't always how it seems. And the kicker is, I'm up to speed now, but if I don't stay on track with the Byrne project and whatever else comes my way afterwards..." I shrug. "The truth is, if I've learnt anything this past month, it's that I can't do this on my own. Never could."

"That's not true, you just have to adapt."

"I'm a terrible manager, I know that now. Neeraj has been asking about you. Forget that, even *Byrne,* when I set up a meeting for Monday wanted to know if you'd be there. Cleary told him about you. Before, when I had Akhil, I didn't appreciate this fact, everything just worked out. But it became painfully obvious after I failed to take over and you agreed to help. Meetings, presentations, getting contracts signed, and the design side of things are all fine. But I can't for the life of me manage a group of stubborn programmers." I wipe my eyes with the back of my hand. "I wish things were different, really. All I've ever wanted was to be independent, to prove that I could be a success without Dad launching my career. But I just can't. I've failed."

The silence resulting from my outburst and confession grows until it threatens to swallow me and the entire room whole.

"I can't believe you're broke." George shakes his head.

After minutes of silence, a smile forms on his lips and he starts to chuckle.

Then that chuckle turns louder, into a laugh, until he can't contain himself anymore and infects me too.

He walks over, sits down beside me and rests his face in his hands and we both laugh uncontrollably, until tears stream down my face again.

"And I thought-" He turns towards me, allowing our eyes to meet. "Oh God. This is tragic."

We burst out laughing again.

"I didn't want to tell you about the bank because I was worried about what you'd think!" I confess, in between further giggles.

Funny, how sometimes the saddest things can tickle you the most. Minutes pass before either of us calm down enough to break the cycle.

"Now what?" He looks over at me with those steely eyes that have haunted my imagination since the first time we met.

"You tell me. What do you want?" I ask. "Do you think we can get past this?"

He doesn't answer, instead just continues to stare into my eyes, silencing me as well. After what feels like forever, he leans towards me, his arm outstretched. I gladly accept the gesture, falling into his embrace and resting my face on his shoulder. I don't know what will happen between us now, I just know I want to feel him close to me. His touch on my skin, his lips against mine, all of which make me choke up again.

I need him now, even if it's the last time. And especially if it's the first of a new beginning.

CHAPTER SEVENTEEN

As it turns out, we could get past it.

Of course, relationships aren't always a smooth ride. We both knew that going into it, even if we lacked a lot of practical experience. And honesty really does need to come first.

It's been a few weeks since our big fight and reconciliation, and after a long day working on Callum Byrne's website project, we find ourselves having to do something other than ordering takeout.

The date of my birthday party crept up on me almost without warning, but tonight is the night.

A few days after we both came clean, George did move out of his old place, and used the profit share from the Cleary deal on a deposit for a place in Reading itself, greatly reducing the daily commute to come here. In truth though, he stays over quite a lot, and over the weekends, we've been taking a break from the computer by doing up his new place together, spending the initial night together on a mattress on the floor.

It felt like such an adventure, camping in his new flat. The beginning of a new chapter for either of us.

He still thinks my house is too big, and he may

have a point there. Although he has gotten used to the big TV, he is a man after all, who likes his toys.

"Luce, just exactly how formal is this birthday thing going to be?" George asks, while unpacking an overnight bag with fresh laundry he's brought from home.

"Just wear whatever you want, I know I will."

With a bit of luck, the weather will hold up, meaning we will get access to the club lawn as well. For the first time in quite a while, I'm actually looking forward to a birthday party.

In between picking out shoes to match my dress, I send a quick message to Dad, making sure he's bringing what I asked him for. The response is almost instant; he's got it, I need not worry.

"Still, if I'm going to meet your parents, I should at least make a bit of an effort, don't you think?" George wonders.

"Relax, they'll love you once they get to know you." I put the phone away again, smiling to myself.

"You think so?"

"I know so. I know I do." It slips out before I can analyze what I'm saying, but George catches it straightaway and leaves the bag, the clothes, whatever he's doing and walks over.

"You what?" He guides my face upwards, staring straight down into my eyes.

It still overwhelms me, the beautiful tension, that

can only be broken with the right kind of physical contact. I blink a few times, trying to find the nerve to truly open up.

"I love you," I whisper, while my knees threaten to buckle.

This look of his, when he's so close to me, so close that we both find it hard to focus on anything other than our most primal instincts, this is what I crave. A look that truly sees me for me. He doesn't see a bit of fun for Friday night. He doesn't see the workaholic who felt her business was more important than making a true connection in life.

Me. *His.*

He runs his thumb over my chin, and I fight with everything I've got to keep my eyes open and prolong the moment. As long as I really pay attention to what's there, in his eyes, I'll always feel safe.

"I love you too." His voice sounds rough, making me wonder what he's thinking. If he's ever said this to someone else, and gotten hurt. But it doesn't matter, because I won't hurt him, not anymore.

Finally, I can't keep my composure anymore, and am forced to blink.

He places his hands on my hips, and bends down until I'm able to reach his lips with mine. That first kiss always does the trick, driving me crazy, making me want infinitely more.

I start to float, literally, as he lifts me, allowing me

to wrap both legs and arms around him tightly.

"You know, if you do want to impress my folks, perhaps we shouldn't be late..."

"I hate it when you're all practical."

"And right?"

He nods, staring into my eyes deeply, which once again gives me shivers. I don't want to release him, instead I want to see where this will go, but we really do have to get dressed if we want to make it.

When he releases me, I almost want to scream at him for listening. But I don't, instead I focus on putting on a pair of stockings and then the dress I'd picked out earlier. Behind me, he's most definitely watching, which puts me on edge. Patience... we'll get our chance, later. We always do.

Tonight will definitely start off a little weird, when I introduce George to my folks, but they'll come around soon enough. It's not every day that I turn up with a plus-one, in fact I don't remember the last time it's happened at all.

***

As it turned out, things were a lot less awkward than I'd anticipated. After scrutinizing him only for a couple of seconds, Mum accepted George for the sweet, kind soul that he is inside. Dad took just a little longer, insisting on asking professional questions, which he aced, of course. I'd gotten a little taste of George dealing with difficult people during the Cleary presentation, and Dad was much easier to win over.

After the initial surprise, Mum especially couldn't contain her excitement that I'd finally met someone special. She literally told George as much, leaving me embarrassed and blushing in the background.

Then Dad took me aside, and after I reassured him I know what I'm doing, handed me what I'd asked him for. A large brown envelope, containing the one thing which I know will ensure things stay perfect between George and me. I tucked it away safely in my bag, now I've just got to find the right time to give it to him.

We mingle for a bit, and sample the food. If there's one thing Mum and Dad know how to do, it's organize a get-together. I'd feel guilty for not helping out at all, if I didn't know deep down Mum loves being in charge of parties. She's always been the perfect hostess.

After introducing George to cousin after cousin, and aunts and uncles, one member of our family remains absent. Perhaps Peter couldn't make it after all. Or Stephanie, his wife might have thrown a spanner in the works. Despite his absence, it's still a nice party.

"I suppose it would be rude to skip out on everyone now, wouldn't it?" George asks, bringing me back to reality.

I let out a laugh. "Definitely. But I suppose we could hide out in that pavilion over there for a while, until people take notice."

He follows my gaze across the lush green lawn of the club. The old-fashioned gazebo, surrounded by large rhododendron shrubs in full bloom, looks like a setting taken right out of a romance movie. Despite still being overlooked—it has open sides after all—it's more private than where we are right now, next to the buffet table, so off we go.

"I know you said you didn't want a gift, but I got you a little something anyway. Happy birthday, Lucy." George wraps his arm around me, as soon as we step up into the pavilion.

"Oh?" I turn to face him, unable to hide my excitement. I didn't expect a gift, actually the fact that we managed to talk things through and decided to try again was more than enough of a gift to me.

"Well, it's more something for the both of us to enjoy together..." He hands me an envelope, which I accept with a slight tremble in my fingers.

I open the flap, and pull out a black, shiny slip of paper. It's a ticket to a music festival. It takes me a while to scan through the various logos on the back, but there it is: Blind Guardian. It was one of the first things we discovered about one another, that we share the same favorite band.

ONE NIGHT STAND

"Perhaps we can make a ride out of it?" George suggests.

I knew he'd seen them live before, I hadn't. There isn't much fun in going to a music concert on your own, but now I've got both the necessary ticket and the perfect company.

"Thank you," I whisper, shooting him a smile, before examining the ticket again.

The concert may be a couple of months away, but that's not what catches my attention. Rather, it's the booking date... It's dated the day of the Cleary presentation. My eyes moisten at the realization.

"You've been keeping this a while, eh?" I ask.

"I may have been broke, but I couldn't very well ignore your birthday once I found out about it."

"What if it hadn't worked out? What if you'd actually left like you said you would?"

He shrugs, and avoids eye contact, almost making me regret bringing up that painful memory.

"I was going to post it to you along with my ticket. I wouldn't have wanted to go on my own."

That admission pushes me over the edge, causing a lone tear to drip down from my lashes, and roll down my cheek.

"I wouldn't have wanted to either," I whisper.

"Hey! Don't cry now, you're supposed to be happy, celebrating." George cups my face with his hands, and wipes the tear away with his thumb.

"I've got something for you too," I say.

"That's funny, seeing as my birthday isn't for another three months," George jokes, releasing me.

I retrieve the A4-sized envelope Dad had given me earlier from my bag and hand it to him.

"Here." I wait, my heart once again beating in my throat, even though this time I'm pretty sure I'm on the right track. There is no way this particular decision will misfire. *I hope.*

"Well, this sure doesn't look like gig tickets." George gives me a questioning look, before tearing open the envelope and pulling out a thick stack of papers, held together with a paper clip.

I give him a moment to read the front.

"This is..." He pauses, reading it again.

"A partnership agreement."

"Why?" He looks up, the surprise still evident in his face.

"Like we talked about, you being my employee is hardly a good basis for a relationship. And I can't do this alone, so..."

"You would do this? Make me a partner in your business? After you worked so hard to build it up from scratch?"

"Everything, including the business, is so much better when you're a part of it. So, yes. If you want."

George puts the contract down on top of the circular bench lining the edge of the gazebo, and takes me into his arms.

"You're quite something, Lucy, I don't know what to say."

I hang on to him, tightly. This closeness with him, this newfound honesty, is making me feel safer than I've ever felt, even while taking what could be seen as a massive risk.

"Then say yes," I whisper, before leaning back just enough to be able to look him in the eye. "Will you be my partner? In this as well as in life?"

"Of course."

We embrace again, neither of us in a hurry to let go.

"I love you," George whispers, his deep voice tickling me to my core.

"I love you too."

****

AUTHOR'S NOTE

Firstly, thanks so much for reading One Night Stand!

This novella has been quite a long time coming. You see, it all started in March 2013 when I released a short story called Just for One Night. That little story, which I intended to be a stand-alone snapshot of two people finding each other in a pub, has now grown to 3 times its original length. I always knew Lucy and George's story wouldn't end after their one night stand, but I didn't get the chance to write about it until the beginning of 2015. Now, in the latter half of 2016, I've decided to relaunch this story as well as the others in the series.

Much like my other work, One Night Stand also deals with regular people, whose love life is often less than perfect. In this case, everything started out well enough when Lucy and George first meet. But after a fantastic, almost surreal and passionate night together, real life inevitably kicks in. What we're left with is control freak Lucy, who has never needed anyone in her life, suddenly coming to terms with the idea that perhaps life is better when you're not on your own. And George, who may look tough and imposing on the outside, struggling with a whole host of his own issues, not least of which the perceived imbalance between his own (professional) worth compared to Lucy's.

Although it's romantic to think that money (especially when one person has way more than the other) should not affect relationships, the opposite is often true. Even the most enlightened, forward-thinking man can feel inferior when faced with a woman who is seemingly so much more successful than he is. He may admire her, even love her, but it's hard to completely break free of the societal norms which expect that a man should take on the role of breadwinner in a household. It can be emasculating. And to then start working together, not as a team, but as boss and employee can really amp up the conflict.

Luckily, Lucy and George are able to save what they have because they adjust. Lucy accepts that she didn't just need George's help temporarily, before taking back control of her business and her life for herself. And when she confesses her dire financial situation to him, he realizes she's not as perfect as he thought she was, which actually makes her more lovable. She not only lets him in on her secret, but creates a situation where both of them can help each other, not as boss and employee, but as partners.

Anyway, I hope you got some pleasure out of this story. Feel free to connect or get in touch via email or social media; I do my best to answer every message I get as soon as possible!

x, Lorelei

- ❖ LMoone.com
- ❖ Lorelei Moone on Facebook
- ❖ AuthorLMoone on Instagram

I also write Paranormal Romance as Lorelei Moone. Check out LoreleiMoone.com for more information.

SPECIAL OFFER!

For a limited time, all new mailing list subscribers will receive a FREE short story, called At First Sight.

Claim your free copy here:

LMoone.com

Look for the newsletter sign-up form on the right hand side of the page.

YOUR NEXT READ?

One Night Stand isn't the only big boy romance book I've written over the years.

I'm actually starting a new series, called Big Boys Do It Better, which is going to release throughout 2021.

Check out the first book below:

RECIPE FOR PASSION

A man who makes food like this… has got to be an amazing lover.

I've landed the job of a lifetime: to write a profile about the Heartthrob Chef himself, Byron Ainsworth. Too bad he's a slime ball in person. No, the real hero on the set of Decadent Desserts is Ethan, Byron's deliciously cuddly sous-chef, and I'm making it my mission to spend my time at the studio mostly with him. Let's call it background research.

As I enjoy more of Ethan's company and my article begins to take shape, I realize two things: I need to tell Ethan how I feel about him before it's too late. And something feels wrong about Byron. I just don't know what it is yet.

Available to order from all major book retailers - ISBN: 9781913930547

Bloody typical. Day one at the new job, and I'm crushing so hard on my colleague I can't think straight.

John isn't your average romance novel hero. He doesn't have a way with the ladies, neither does he have six pack abs. He's just a regular guy with a bit of a dad bod, and he's shy and awkward rather than suave and charming.

That's cool, because I'm just a regular girl. One who's already head over heels for him and he doesn't even realise it...

Available to order from all major book retailers - ISBN: 9781913930028

OTHER PUBLICATIONS

<u>Big Boys Do It Better Series:</u>
Recipe for Passion
Paperback ISBN: 9781913930547
Best Friends Forever
Paperback ISBN: 9781913930554

<u>The Chance Encounters Series:</u>
One Night Stand
Paperback ISBN: 9781913930080
Beautiful Stranger
Paperback ISBN: 9781913930103
Only a Taste
Paperback ISBN: 9781913930127

<u>The Undateables Series:</u>
The Rebound List
Paperback ISBN: 9781913930042
Sally
Paperback ISBN: 9781913930066

<u>As Lorelei Moone:</u>
<u>The Scottish Werebears Series:</u>
An Unexpected Affair
Paperback ISBN: 9781913930165
A Dangerous Business
Paperback ISBN: 9781913930172
A Forbidden Love
Paperback ISBN: 9781913930189
A New Beginning
Paperback ISBN: 9781913930196
A Painful Dilemma
Paperback ISBN: 9781913930202
A Second Chance
Paperback ISBN: 9781913930219

<u>The Alpha Squad Series:</u>
Boot Camp
Paperback ISBN: 9781913930233
Friends & Foes
Paperback ISBN: 9781913930240
Infiltrator
Paperback ISBN: 9781913930257
Showdown
Paperback ISBN: 9781913930264

The Vampires of London Series:

Alexander's Blood Bride
Paperback ISBN: 9781913930288

Michael's Soul Mate
Paperback ISBN: 9781913930295

Lucille's Valentine
Paperback ISBN: 9781913930301

The Shifters of Black Isle Series:

Claimed by the King
Paperback ISBN: 9781913930325

The Soldier and the Siren
Paperback ISBN: 9781913930332

A Dragon's Treasure
Paperback ISBN: 9781913930349

The Warlock's Conquest
Paperback ISBN: 9781913930356